HOME COMFORTS AT ROOKERY HOUSE

ROSIE HENDRY

Home Comforts at Rookery House

Published by Rookery House Press
Cover design by designforwriters.com

For Sue Baker,
with love and thanks for all her wonderful
support for readers and writers.

CHAPTER 1

Early February 1942 – Great Plumstead, Norfolk

'Can you help? Please.'

Prue Wilson listened to Group Captain Barlow's deep voice coming down the telephone wire from the newly opened RAF Great Plumstead and wondered if this was a request too far.

In her role as the local billeting officer, this wasn't the first time Prue had suddenly been asked to find accommodation in the village but, with the influx of so many people since the start of the war, the place was bursting at the seams. She couldn't see how there was room for any more people to stay.

'I'm not…' she began.

'But it is *only* for a couple of weeks!' the Group Captain butted in. 'Three at the most. It's just until the new accommodation is finished. The Waafs will need space to park a camp bed each, somewhere to do their ablutions and have breakfast, that's all. The remainder of the time they'll be here at the aerodrome and will have their other meals in our cookhouse. We can supply camp beds and bedding. All that's needed is room to put them up. Please Mrs Wilson, can you find a billet for them? I have been reliably informed that you're *the* person around here who can get things done.'

'All right, I'll see what I can do. But we've had so many people move into the village since the start of the war I'm not sure there are any spare bedrooms left anywhere,' Prue warned him. 'I will try to find somewhere for your Waafs, but I can't guarantee I'll find anything. You may end up having to look further afield.'

'Excellent! I have every faith in you, Mrs Wilson,' Group Captain Barlow said optimistically.

'You haven't told me when you want the billets for,' Prue said.

'Oh, didn't I say? It's tomorrow. The Waafs are arriving on a transport tomorrow afternoon.' He gave a chuckle and before Prue could respond he added, 'I look forward to hearing from you.' Then he quickly disconnected the call.

Prue stood open-mouthed, the receiver still held to her ear, thinking he'd just well and truly pulled the wool over her eyes. If she didn't sort this problem out, then three Waafs would arrive at RAF Great Plumstead tomorrow only to find themselves kipping in one of the draughty hangars and washing in puddles!

Her supposedly quiet Sunday evening at home felt like it had just had a firework explode in it, Prue thought, replacing the black Bakelite receiver on to its cradle. Somehow she must help these young women because she didn't like the thought of what might happen to them otherwise.

Prue returned to the sitting room where she'd been playing cards with her eighteen-year-old daughter Alice, before the telephone ringing out in the hall had interrupted their game.

'Who was that?' Alice asked from her seat in one of the armchairs by the fire, her hand of cards laid on the little table pulled up between hers and the chair opposite.

'It was Group Captain Barlow from RAF Great Plumstead. He wants me to find billets for three Waafs for a few weeks until their accommodation is finished. The building of it is behind schedule apparently.'

Alice leaned forward. 'You can do that, can't you, Ma? You're good at finding places for people to stay.'

'Normally it's not such a problem.' Prue sat down opposite her daughter. 'But I think the village is already at capacity. And the Waafs are arriving tomorrow.'

'Tomorrow!' Alice exclaimed. 'That's a bit short notice, isn't it?'

'I know, but he's told me they only need space to set up a camp bed somewhere. Most of the time, they'll be at the aerodrome. I suppose, if it's necessary, they could sleep in the village hall. There's a kitchen there, lavatories and sinks for a wash. It would be better than sleeping in a hangar, which might be their only option if I can't find them anywhere else to stay.'

'We could put one up here. I'm willing to share my bedroom with a Waaf,' Alice said. 'It's only for a few weeks, and if they're bringing a camp bed with them, we could easily fit it in my room. It would give me a chance to talk to them and get to know what life's really like serving in the WAAF. I've been wondering if it's the sort of thing I'd like to do.' Alice looked at Prue, her blue eyes bright with eagerness. 'What do you think? We could manage with one more person in the house, couldn't we? After all, we made room for Nancy and the girls, didn't we?'

'Yes, we did, and it's been a pleasure to have them staying with us,' Prue agreed.

Nancy, who was upstairs supervising her children having a bath, was an evacuee from the East End of London. Her home had been destroyed in the Blitz and she'd come to live here with her two young daughters, Marie and Joan, in the autumn of 1940. They'd settled in well and Nancy had become a good friend to Prue. Although the same couldn't be said of Prue's husband, Victor, who hated having strangers living in his house, but with spare rooms and the law requiring them to be given to evacuees, he'd had no choice but to accept the situation.

'What do you think, Ma? The conscription age for women is bound to change sooner or later and I'll get called up and put wherever I'm sent. If I can decide soon and volunteer, then I can choose what I do. I don't want to end up indoors all day in a munitions factory! Plus, if we can put a Waaf up for a couple of weeks, it's one less billet you've got to find,' Alice said in an encouraging tone.

Prue looked at her daughter and smiled. 'You're right. For both reasons. Very well then, if you're happy to share your room, then we'll have one Waaf stay here with us. But that still leaves me with two billets to find.'

'Aunt Thea might help,' Alice suggested.

'She hasn't got any spare bedrooms at Rookery House now,' Prue reminded her daughter.

'No, but if it was a choice between having Waafs sleeping in a cold hangar or putting up a camp bed for a few nights at one end of her dining room, I think she'd offer them a place to stay. You don't know unless you ask, do you?' Alice raised her eyebrows, a smile playing on her lips.

Prue let out a laugh, shaking her head. 'Very well, I'll go and telephone Thea, see if she can squeeze a Waaf into Rookery House. While I'm doing that, you can think of who else might help with our third one.'

4

CHAPTER 2

Rookery House, Great Plumstead

Thea crouched in the doorway to the bedroom part of the pigsty, watching with a fond smile on her face as the two piglets snuggled themselves down. They lay side by side with most of their bodies buried under the clean straw, which glowed a pale golden-yellow in the light from Thea's Tilley lamp. With just their noses and the top of their heads showing, the piglets were cosily tucked up for the night.

This was the third lot of pigs they'd kept here at Rookery House. Both previous sets had been a great success at turning foods like vegetable scraps, acorns and the leftover whey from Hettie's cheese-making into home-reared meat. This pair had only arrived three days ago but were settling in well and seemed content and calm in their new home.

Standing up, Thea closed the pigsty bedroom door, shutting the piglets in for the night and sheltering them from the icy air. A frost was forming and Thea's breath clouded in the pool of light from the lamp. Overhead, the clear, inky-black sky was peppered with thousands of yellow pinprick stars.

'Thea?'

Turning at the sound of her name, Thea saw the glow of a shielded torch and made out Flo, the Land Girl who worked with her here at Rookery House.

'Prue's on the telephone, wants to talk to you.'

'Did she say what about?' Thea stepped out of the yard part of the pigsty and fastened the gate securely behind her. 'Perhaps we've been ordered to take the WVS canteen somewhere tomorrow. I haven't checked on Primrose yet. Could you please do that for me, while I go and find out what my sister wants?'

'Of course,' Flo replied.

'Thanks. I've already checked the hens and rabbits; it's just Primrose left to do. You take the Tilley lamp with you so you can see what you're doing better.' Thea handed it to Flo, swapping it for the torch, and headed indoors.

After kicking off her rubber boots in the scullery and washing her hands, Thea hurried through to the hall where Hettie was talking on the telephone. The older woman gave Thea a brief nod and spoke into the receiver.

'Thea's here now so I'll see you at The Mother's Day Club on Tuesday.' Hettie handed Thea the receiver and headed back into the sitting room, closing the door softly behind her.

'Hello Prue, what is it? An extra shift with the canteen?' Thea asked.

'No, not this time. I have got another request for you though. I've been given the job of finding temporary billets for three Waafs because their accommodation on the aerodrome isn't ready yet. It's only for two to three weeks and all they need is space to set up a camp bed, have a wash and some breakfast. The rest of the time they'll be at RAF Great Plumstead. I've found a billet for one — well, Alice has kindly volunteered to share her bedroom. I wondered if you could possibly squeeze a Waaf in somewhere? She'd bring her own camp bed and bedding so you wouldn't have to organise that. It's not for long. What do you think?' Prue sounded hopeful.

Thea considered for a moment, hooking a length of her curly brown, jaw-length hair behind her ear. There wasn't a spare bedroom at Rookery House now. She and Hettie had one each. Evie and Flo shared a room. Marianne had both her young daughters in with her. And their evacuee children, George and Betty, had a room between them. Now, whenever anyone came to stay here, they had to sleep on a camp bed in the dining room. So a Waaf or two, especially if it was only for a few weeks, could do that, Thea decided.

'I can help,' Thea said. 'There's space in the dining room they could use.'

'*They?*' Prue asked.

Thea gave a laugh. 'Yes, why not? If we push the table over to the far end there's room enough for two beds. We'll put up *both* the Waafs so there's no need for you to go looking elsewhere for another billet.'

'You will!' Prue exclaimed with delight down the phone line. 'Thank you so much. I was worried I wouldn't find anywhere for them with the village already being so full. I'd considered the village hall as a last option if I didn't have any luck elsewhere. The Group Captain put me in a tight corner, but with you and Alice volunteering, we'll show him what the women of Great Plumstead can do when called on to help.'

'When are they coming?' Thea asked. 'You didn't tell me that.'

'Tomorrow afternoon! That's the thing. He only telephoned ten minutes ago to ask me to find billets, with less than twenty-four hours' notice! Still, we've risen to the occasion. Thank you, I appreciate it,' Prue said. 'I'll telephone the Group Captain now and let him know.'

After they'd said their goodbyes, Thea headed into the sitting room, where the fire burning brightly in the grate was radiating a welcome warmth.

'Is everything all right?' Hettie asked, looking up at Thea, while her hands carried on knitting the sock she was making.

'Yes and I have some news.' She glanced around at Evie, George and Betty who'd paused their game of snakes and ladders at the small table and were all staring at her waiting to hear what she had to tell them.

'What is it?' Marianne asked from the armchair opposite Hettie.

Before Thea could answer, the door opened and Flo came in, her cheeks rosy from the cold outside.

'You're just in time to hear the news, Flo. We're going to have two Waafs come to live with us for a few weeks,' Thea announced. 'Prue's been tasked with finding billets for three. She's having one stay at hers and I've said we'll have the other two here.'

'But where are we going to put them?' Hettie asked.

'In the dining room. They're bringing their own camp beds and bedding. If we push the table over to the far end, then there'll be enough space. I thought, if you're not doing any sewing commissions at the moment, Marianne, it won't matter too much if the table's tucked away for a bit.'

'That's fine,' agreed Marianne. 'I don't think I'll be taking any on for a good while yet. Looking after baby Bea and Emily keeps me busy enough.'

'With you getting up several times in the night to feed Bea, you're tired enough as it is,' Hettie added, a concerned look on her face. 'The sewing will still be there when you're ready to begin again.'

Marianne gave the older woman a smile. 'Looking after my girls is the most important thing for me to do until Alex comes home.'

Thea's heart went out to the young woman who, since her evacuation here as an expectant mother at the start of the war, had become like family to Thea and everyone else at Rookery House. Last November, Marianne's husband Alex had been posted as Missing In Action after his plane had gone down. He'd been lucky to survive and was now being held as a Prisoner of War in a German prison camp.

'What's a Waaf?' George piped up.

Thea turned her attention to the six-year-old who, with his eight-year-old sister Betty had been evacuated to another billet in the village during the London Blitz, and then came to stay here at Rookery House after their mother returned home to the East End.

'A Waaf is a woman who serves in the Royal Air Force,' Thea explained.

'Waaf stands for Women's Auxiliary Air Force,' Flo said, sitting down next to George. 'Are they coming to work at RAF Great Plumstead?' she asked Thea.

'Yes, but their accommodation isn't ready. That's why Prue's been given the job of finding them somewhere to stay. They'll be at the aerodrome most of the time and only have breakfast here and sleep, of course.'

'Will they fly aeroplanes?' Betty asked, eagerly.

'I don't think so. Anyway, the planes haven't arrived yet. These must be an advance group of Waafs helping to get things organised ahead of the rest of the servicemen and women arriving. We'll be able to ask them about what's happening at the aerodrome,' Thea said. 'It will be fascinating to find out more about it as there's only so much we can see from the road and we're not allowed on there.'

'What time will they be here?' Hettie asked.

'Sometime tomorrow afternoon, that's all I know,' Thea replied. 'We'll get the room ready in the morning. It shouldn't take long. If they're bringing their own beds they can set them up when they arrive.'

'We could stay off school tomorrow, then we'll be at home when they get here to welcome them,' Betty suggested.

Thea glanced at Hettie, who raised her eyebrows behind her round glasses at the little girl's suggestion.

'No, it's important you go to school for your education. Your mother wouldn't want you missing it. The Waafs should be here waiting when you get home.' Thea gave the little girl a reassuring smile. 'You'll be able to ask them lots of questions.'

'Can I show them the animals?' George asked.

Thea nodded. 'Of course you can, you and Betty. That will be nice for you all.'

Thea smiled to herself. Coming to stay here at Rookery House was going to be quite a change from what the Waafs would have been used to living on other aerodromes. She hoped they'd liked it!

CHAPTER 3

Watching the flickering orange and gold flames burning in the grate reminded Prue of her childhood, when she'd often sat by the hearth staring into it.

She loved how the fire constantly changed, the embers glowing as if alive and the flames dancing. Her mother had told her to look for pictures, see what she could see. Prue still did that. She enjoyed the comforting noises – the gentle snap and flutter as the logs burned, the creaks as they shifted on the grate, sounds that always gave her a deep sense of comfort and peace. And Prue needed that right now as she waited for her husband to return so she could tell him that a Waaf would be coming to stay with them. Judging by his previous reactions to having people come to live in their home because of the war, she knew it wouldn't go down well.

Prue was alone downstairs. Nancy had gone up to bed a short while ago and Alice not long after. Victor was late tonight. The time he returned from his so-called Sunday meetings in Norwich varied but, seeing as it was now almost ten o'clock, she suspected he'd probably got the last train back and should be here soon.

It didn't bother Prue that he was late. In fact, she preferred it. If Victor wanted to spend longer with his mistress, it was fine with Prue. Life here at home was far better when her husband wasn't around to spoil things with his nasty temper and mean ways.

The sound of the front door opening and closing announced his arrival. Prue could picture him in the hall, taking off his coat and hat and hanging them precisely on the coat stand. She smoothed down her ash-blonde hair, checking it was still neat in its soft roll at the back of her head and then braced herself. Prue knew he'd come straight into the sitting room, thinking someone had left a light on rather than that anyone had stayed up to greet him. Usually if he was this late coming home, Prue would already have gone up to her bedroom to save herself from having to see him until breakfast the next morning.

'Oh, it's you, Prudence!' Victor's voice cut through the air. 'What are you doing still up?'

She looked at him standing in the doorway and squeezed her hands into fists on her lap in the last few calm moments before the storm. She knew it would come as surely as night follows day.

'I have some news.' She forced her voice to remain steady while inside her heart picked up its pace. 'Group Captain Barlow from RAF Great Plumstead has asked me to find billets for three Waafs. It's just for a few weeks until their accommodation is ready.'

'Well we can't have any here! We don't have the room,' Victor snapped. 'You've already given away *two* bedrooms to that East End woman and her brats.' Victor came further into the room, glaring down at her, his ice-blue eyes narrowed.

Prue inwardly flinched at the way he talked about Nancy. She knew he wouldn't say that in front of her friend because she'd give him short shrift, but like all bullies, Victor was quick to be unkind if he thought he was safe.

'Actually we're having *one* Waaf stay here…,' Prue began.

'No! No! No!' Victor punctuated his words with stabs of his finger on the back of an armchair. 'This is *my* house and *I* decide who stays here, not you, Prudence.'

'It was Alice who volunteered to share her room with a Waaf. It's not for long. And as billeting officer, I have a duty to do what I can to help, as do *you*, seeing as you're chair of the village hall committee and member of the Home Guard along with your various other committees and meetings. It's *our* responsibility to do what we can in times of need. The Group Captain gave me short notice as the Waafs are arriving tomorrow.' She looked him straight in the eye. 'Thea's having *two* Waafs staying with her.'

Victor's mouth thinned into a line beneath his thin, bristly moustache and he sniffed as if an unpleasant smell had materialised under his nose. A reaction, Prue was certain, to the mention of Thea and the fact that she was helping with two Waafs. Victor disliked Thea almost as much as Thea disliked him.

'This is *my* house!' Victor hissed, taking a menacing step towards Prue. 'It's up to *me* who stays here, not you!' He jabbed his finger at her.

'Ma? Is everything all right?'

They both turned their heads to see Alice standing in the doorway, dressed in her dressing gown and slippers, her long blonde hair woven into a plait that hung over one shoulder. 'I heard raised voices.' She advanced into the room.

'I was just telling your father about the Waaf who's coming to stay,' Prue said.

Alice smiled at her father. 'Oh, I'm so much looking forward to it! Although the Waaf won't be here much from what the Group Captain told Ma, just here to sleep and have breakfast. The rest of the time she'll be at the aerodrome. You'll hardly know she's here, Father.'

Victor turned to his daughter; his brow creased in furrows of disapproval. 'Did your mother put you up to sharing a room with a stranger?'

'No! Of course not. I *volunteered*. It was my idea.' Alice met her father's icy gaze with her own warmer blue eyes. 'We've all got to do our bit to help the war effort in whatever way we can. Look at what you do, Father. You even spend your Sundays at committee meetings in Norwich each week instead of having a rest from work at home. You help in the way you can. My sharing a room for a couple of weeks is me doing my bit too. I know it's not much but every little thing helps.'

Prue bit the inside of her cheek to stop herself from letting out a snort of laughter at what her daughter had just said. What would Alice say if she knew that the only meeting her father had each Sunday was with his mistress?

'You're right,' Victor acknowledged, puffing up his chest. 'We must all do what we can, no matter how small it is. Every little thing does help. Although in future I want to be consulted first about strangers coming to stay in *my home*.' He turned to glare at Prue as he delivered this last line.

'Time was of the essence in this case,' Prue said. 'And you weren't here to ask.'

Victor narrowed his eyes at her for a moment before announcing, 'I'm going to bed.' Without even another look at Prue, he gave his daughter the briefest touch on her shoulder and left the room.

Prue let out a sigh as she heard his heavy tread going up the stairs, her shoulders relaxing with relief.

'Are you all right, Ma?' Alice asked, coming over to sit on the arm of Prue's chair and putting an arm around her. 'We're doing the right thing helping out. It's not as if the Waaf is moving in long term. Honestly, Father sounds so pompous sometimes with his *my house* business. It's *our* family home; it's not just Father that lives here. You're the one who keeps the place running, makes sure we have meals to eat, clean clothes to wear. If it was left to him, everything would fall apart. He should appreciate all you do, Ma.'

Prue took hold of her daughter's hand. 'I don't think that's ever likely to happen. And I don't want his appreciation. There are plenty of other people and things in my life that matter more to me than getting his approval.'

'Well, I'm proud of all you do. You've done so much to help people in this village,' Alice said. 'You get things done when help's needed. That matters.'

Prue glanced up at her daughter and smiled. 'Thank you, I appreciate *you* saying so.' She gave Alice's hand a squeeze. 'Now we'd better go to bed. You're due at work at Thea's in the morning and I've got to get things ready for the Waaf. I'll need to move the furniture around in your bedroom a bit to make space for a camp bed.'

They both stood up and Prue pulled Alice into a hug, making the most of being able to do so while her daughter was still here. After what Alice had said earlier about volunteering before conscription came in, she feared that her days left at home were numbered.

CHAPTER 4

'There, I think that's everything, and if it isn't, we can soon sort it out,' Hettie said, hands on her hips as she surveyed the dining room at Rookery House.

Thea and Flo had moved the table to the far end of the room earlier, leaving space for the Waafs to set up their camp beds. Hettie and Marianne had dusted, swept and polished in here and now the dining room was ready for its new occupants who'd be arriving sometime this afternoon.

'I'm sure they'll be comfy in here and will probably be glad to only have to share it with each other,' Marianne said.

'I'm sure they will,' Hettie agreed. 'Grace Barker told me her daughter's sharing a Nissen hut with eleven other Waafs. I think staying here at Rookery House will be a treat for them. It's certainly more homely than a Nissen hut!'

The rattle of the letter box in the front door signalled the arrival of the morning post.

'Me get?' asked two-year-old Emily, looking up at Marianne with a hopeful expression.

'Go on then, you can fetch the post.' Marianne laughed as her eldest daughter raced to the front door.

'Emily does love fetching the post now,' Hettie said, fondly.

'I think she understands how much it means for us to get a letter from Alex.' Marianne gave a faltering smile. 'It's our only contact with him while he's in the camp and it's a lifeline to us all.'

Hettie put her hand on Marianne's arm. 'It's hard for you all. But your letters to each other keep you in touch and your strong bond going, no matter how far you are apart right now.'

Marianne nodded, blinking away tears as her daughter came hurrying into the room holding several envelopes in her small hands.

'Let's see who they're for.' Marianne took the letters the little girl handed to her. 'There's one for you.' She passed it to Hettie. 'And one for Flo, and look…' She held the third one out for her daughter to see. 'There's one for us, Emily! It's from your daddy.'

The little girl beamed with delight at the news. 'Open now?'

'That's a lovely way to start your week. You two go and read it and I'll finish up in here,' Hettie said. 'I just want to open the window for a bit and let the fresh air blow through.'

Marianne nodded her thanks. 'Come on, Emily.' She held out her hand to her daughter. 'Let's go and read our precious letter.'

After they'd gone, Hettie pulled the top sash window down, letting in the crisp February air. Then she headed through to the kitchen to read her own letter. She hadn't recognised the handwriting and, with its London postmark, Hettie had no idea who it was from.

After checking on baby Bea, who was fast asleep in the pram parked by the dresser, Hettie sat down at the table and opened the envelope. Taking out the letter, she unfolded the single sheet of paper and looked at the signature at the bottom… Lucille Brown. She was Hettie's great-niece and granddaughter of her brother Sidney who'd emigrated to Canada many years ago. Hettie began to read.

Dear Aunt Hettie,

I hope this letter comes as a nice surprise for you. I got your address from Grandpa before I was shipped overseas. I'm now in the Canadian Royal Air Force and working here in London and enjoying being in England. When I have some leave, I'd like to come to Norfolk to see you. I've heard such a lot about you from Grandpa, along with tales of where he grew up. It would be wonderful to see the village and countryside as he always talks of you and the place he lived with great fondness.
Please write back to me and I hope that we can meet one day.

With warmest wishes,

Lucille Brown

Hettie sat back in her chair smiling at the thought of her brother's granddaughter being here in England, and yes, it would be a delight to meet her. She could come and stay here at Rookery House and they could visit Hettie's sister Ada too, who worked as housekeeper up at Great Plumstead Hall. Hettie was already looking forward to showing Lucille around the village and Ivy Cottage where she and her brothers and sister had grown up. It was a long time since Sidney and her other brother, Albert, had gone to live in Canada and sadly they'd never come back for a visit. They had both kept in touch with letters over the years and told Hettie about their marriages, children, and then grandchildren. The prospect of meeting one of Sidney's granddaughters filled Hettie with excitement. Lucille would be most welcome.

A little after three o'clock that afternoon, Hettie heard the rumble of the RAF lorry before she saw it. She was just coming down the stairs when it turned in through the gate and came to a halt in front of the house.

Usually the residents of Rookery House and visitors went around to the back door, but with beds and luggage to be carried in, it would be much easier to open the front door which was near the dining room, Hettie thought, hurrying along the hall to let the new arrivals in.

'Oh, I was just about to knock,' a blonde-haired Waaf declared in a warm Scottish voice, her hand raised. She quickly stuck it out towards Hettie instead. 'I'm Elspeth McBain.'

'Hettie Brown.' Hettie shook the young woman's hand. 'Welcome to Rookery House.'

'This is Marge Taylor.' Elspeth beckoned to a brown-haired Waaf, who stepped forward and shook hands with Hettie.

'Where do you want the beds?' A RAF man asked, hauling a

camp bed out of the back of the lorry and balancing it on one shoulder.

'It's this way,' Hettie said, 'just in here to the left.' She pointed through the open front door.

'We'll get our things.' Elspeth headed back to the lorry.

'Can I help?' Hettie asked.

'No, you're fine,' the RAF man said, striding past her. 'It won't take us long to unload.'

He was right. Between him and the two Waafs, the beds, biscuit mattresses, bedding and their large, white canvas kitbags were soon unloaded and carried into the dining room. The last things off the lorry were two black-framed bicycles with white-painted back mudguards.

'Our transport to the aerodrome,' Marge said, wheeling her bicycle away from the lorry. 'Where shall we store them, Hettie?' she asked.

'Round the back in one of the sheds. I'll show you...' Hettie began but halted at the arrival of Thea with George and Betty, who'd been at school all day.

'You're here!' Betty said in an excited voice.

George grabbed hold of Thea's hand and stood shyly by her side, his eyes wide as he took in the large RAF lorry, two Waafs and the RAF man.

'This is Thea, the owner of Rookery House.'

Hettie quickly introduced the two Waafs. 'I was about to show them where to store their bicycles,' she said.

'We'll show you,' Thea said. 'If you follow us.'

Hettie watched as Thea, with George still holding her hand, led the two women wheeling their bicycles around to the back of the house.

'Will you stop for a cup of tea?' Hettie asked the RAF man.

'Thank you, that's very kind, but I don't have time. There's lots to do getting the aerodrome ready for the full complement of staff to arrive,' he said. 'I've already dropped another Waaf in the village so will be heading straight back to the aerodrome to get on with the next job.'

'You must have met Prue then, when you dropped the other Waaf off; she's Thea's sister,' Hettie told him.

'It's good of you all to put up the Waafs, otherwise they'd have been sleeping in one of the hangars and they're chilly places. Not that the Nissen huts are much warmer!' He gave a laugh and headed for the lorry. 'Nice to meet you.'

Hettie waved him off and went inside, shutting the front door behind her.

Peering into the dining room, it looked smaller with the two camp beds and equipment in there, but it would do for a short time.

'Elspeth says they sleep on biscuits!' Betty declared, marching into the room, closely followed by the two Waafs, Thea and George. 'That's not right, is it, Hettie? You eat biscuits, not sleep on them.'

'It's no fib, I can assure you! See?' Elspeth picked up one of the brown flat square cushions piled on the table. 'This is a biscuit and we have three of them on our bed to make the mattress. And each morning, after we get up, we must stack them on each other, fold the blankets on top of them and wrap them in the sheets.'

'Why?' asked George shyly.

'Because that's what the RAF tells us to do,' Elspeth replied, with a roll of her eyes. 'Once you're a Waaf and in this uniform,' she waved her hand up and down the smart blue tunic and skirt she wore, 'then you have to do as you are told and be ready for inspection.'

'Well you don't have to do it while you're staying with us,' Thea said. 'There'll be no inspections here.'

'We're in the habit now,' Marge said. 'So we'd better keep

doing it while we're here or we might forget once we move onto the aerodrome and get in hot water with our sergeant.'

'I like your blue uniform,' Betty said. 'It's a lovely colour.'

'Thank you.' Marge gave the little girl a beaming smile. 'I think so, too. It's one of the reasons I signed up for the WAAF. I don't like the khaki uniform of the ATS.'

'We'll leave you to settle in and make up your beds and when you're ready, come through to the kitchen and it will be time for tea,' Hettie said.

'We've got some provisions they sent with us.' Elspeth took a cardboard box from the table. 'There's tea in here, sugar, biscuits, oats, powered milk and egg. It's to help cover our breakfasts and the Group Captain said to let him know if you want some more while we're here.'

'Thank you,' Hettie said, taking the box. 'That's a great help.'

After they'd eaten their evening meal, when the Waafs had been introduced to Flo, Marianne and her two daughters, the adults sat around the table chatting. All the children were now in bed, tired after the excitement of the Waafs arrival and showing them around.

'You'll meet Evie later,' Thea told them. 'She's a nurse at Great Plumstead Hall Hospital and her shift ends at seven, so she'll be back after that.'

'And Reuben,' Hettie added.

'That's your brother who lives in the railway carriage house?' Elspeth asked. 'You pointed it out to us earlier when we put our bicycles away.'

'Yes, that's right. He said he'd call in later. He works on the Great Plumstead Hall estate,' Thea said.

'Where are you both from?' Flo asked.

'From a farm in a village near Dundee in Scotland,' Elspeth said.

'I'm from Kenilworth near Coventry,' Marge said.

'Were you living there when Coventry was badly bombed?' Thea asked.

'Yes, I hadn't joined up then. I heard the planes flying over us as they came in to attack Coventry. They destroyed so much of the city. Left so many homeless.' Marge's face looked haunted. 'After that raid, hundreds of people came out to Kenilworth to seek refuge. My family took in as many of them as we could fit in our house.' Marge fell silent for a moment before adding, 'The attack on Coventry made me want to do something more to help, so I volunteered for the WAAF.'

'What job do you do as a Waaf?' Marianne asked.

'I work in the office, same as Elspeth and Patsy, who's billeted in the village. We were brought in before the other Waafs arrive to help do the administration, type letters and so on,' Marge explained. 'It's not very exciting, but it is essential work.'

'I like it,' Elspeth said. 'I'm in the warm and dry. After growing up on a farm and out in all weathers, I fully appreciate a job indoors!'

'I'm the opposite,' Flo said. 'Being a Land Girl puts me outside a lot, but I like it. I used to work in an office in Manchester and hated being stuck indoors all day.'

'Each to their own!' Elspeth grinned. 'As long as we're happy doing our work, it helps. We're grateful to you all for putting us up here, aren't we, Marge?' She glanced at her friend, who nodded.

'Yes. Thank you. We're going to enjoy living in a home again for a while,' Marge added.

'You're very welcome.' Thea smiled at the two young

Waafs. 'Sleeping on camp beds in the dining room isn't ideal but it's the only space we have.'

Elspeth held up her hand. 'Don't worry, it's fine, and it already feels like a real treat staying here after being used to living in a Nissen hut. Being able to enjoy some home comforts again is a delight.'

CHAPTER 5

Prue glanced at the empty seat opposite her at the far end of the kitchen table, where Victor always sat, and felt relieved that he wasn't here. He'd telephoned earlier to inform her he had a committee meeting in Wykeham tonight and wouldn't be home for his evening meal, saying that he'd get something to eat at a pub instead. Whether this was true, or if Victor was really going into Norwich to see his mistress, Prue didn't care. However, it did mean that tonight's meal had a much happier atmosphere than it would have done had Victor been here.

Turning her attention to Nancy and her daughters, nine-year-old Marie and eight-year-old Joan, Alice, and Patsy, the newly arrived Waaf, Prue felt her spirits rising at the cheerful companionship filling the room.

'Me dad works down the mine,' Patsy said in her lovely lilting County Durham accent. 'That's where I'd have ended up working if I'd been a boy. So just as well I was born a girl then, as I would have hated it down there.'

'Is it dark in a mine?' Marie asked, putting down her fork and fixing her gaze on the Waaf.

'Aye. Me dad has to wear a torch on the front of his helmet. Like this,' Patsy said putting her hand to her forehead to mimic a torch's beam, 'that's how he lights his way.'

'How do they get down into the mine?' Joan asked.

'In a cage. It's like a lift and goes down in a deep hole into the ground,' Patsy told her. 'We need the coal for our factories and our fireplaces, don't we? So it has to be dug out by someone.'

Joan nodded.

'Makes you think, though,' Nancy said, 'how much we take coal for granted, not thinking about how it's got out of the ground by men like your dad.'

'Aye.' Patsy agreed. 'Now tell me about yourselves.' She looked around at them all. 'I'm a right nosy parker and love finding out about folk. Being in the WAAF and meeting so many new people from all over has been fascinating. I could tell you some tales about the different lives they've come from.'

'We're from the East End…' Nancy began, telling her story about being bombed out in the Blitz.

Prue smiled to herself as the conversation flew back and forth across the table, with questions and answers, laughter and friendship. There was something joyful about Patsy and the way she lit up a room with her enthusiasm and warmth. From the moment she'd arrived here with her camp bed, kitbag and a bicycle, she had livened up the house with her bubbly, sunny personality and flashing green eyes. Prue had instantly liked the young woman and thought it would be a great pleasure to have her staying. And if tonight's meal was anything to go by, it was going to be fun to have her around for a few weeks. Although Victor wouldn't think so, Prue thought, but then there was very little that he liked or approved of! Prue was past caring what he thought. If the rest of the residents of this house enjoyed Patsy's company that was what mattered.

On her way back from the bathroom as she headed to bed, Prue stopped on the landing outside Alice's bedroom. She could hear Alice and Patsy's voices inside, the pair of them talking before they went to sleep. Prue knew her daughter wanted to ask Patsy about her experience in the WAAF and no doubt was doing just that. It would give her a more realistic view of life in the service and help Alice decide if it was the right thing for her or not.

CHAPTER 6

It was a cold, crisp February morning, a forget-me-not blue sky arching overhead, and the physical work of cutting back and thinning apple tree branches in the orchard was the perfect job to keep warm, Thea thought. Flo and Alice were working on neighbouring trees, each of them pruning vigorous young shoots or overcrowded branches to open up the tree canopy and allow air to circulate better and the sun to reach developing fruits come the summer months.

'How's Patsy settling in?' Thea called across to Alice, curious to know as it had been three days since the Waafs had arrived in the village.

'Very well, she seems happy enough and I'm enjoying having her stay. She's told me loads about being in the WAAF. The basic training and how she had to do a proficiency test so they could work out the best job she was suited to,' Alice said, as she paused in sawing through a thin branch.

'If I'd joined the WAAF, ATS or the Wrens, they'd probably have given me the role of shorthand typist like I was when I worked in the Manchester office,' Flo said, dropping a handful of pruned shoots into the wheelbarrow. 'I didn't want to spend the war doing that! That's one of the reasons I joined the Land Army, but mostly because I love growing things and being outdoors.'

'I'm very glad you made that choice, Flo.' Thea gave the young woman a grateful smile.

'The WAAF uniform is lovely,' Alice said. 'Much better than the ATS's khaki one, and I don't like the hat the Wrens have to wear.'

'Sounds as if you're tempted to join the WAAF then.' Flo snipped through some more shoots with her secateurs.

Thea threw Alice a look, wondering what her niece would say.

'Maybe,' Alice said non-committally. 'It's just a possibility. I'm not rushing into anything without finding out as much as I can about it first. I need to think carefully if it will be the right thing for me or not. Once you sign up, then you're in for the duration of the war and I don't want to be in something I don't like.'

'What does Patsy like about being in the WAAF?' Flo asked.

'Oh all sorts,' Alice said. 'She likes meeting new people, going to different places and having fun with the other Waafs, going out to dances or trips into towns depending on where she's been stationed. Patsy worked at an aerodrome near London for a bit so went into the city whenever she had time off. She likes her job too.'

Thea listened as the pair of them carried on talking about what Alice had found out so far. Despite what her niece had said, Thea could tell that she had more than just a passing interest in joining the WAAF. She'd known it was only a matter of time before Alice left to do something else, as she'd made no secret of her desire to follow her two older brothers and leave home to work for the war effort.

While Thea would be pleased for Alice stepping out of her comfortable, familiar world to gain more experience, go somewhere different and meet many new people, it was going to give Thea a dilemma. She'd have to find someone else to fill Alice's job here at Rookery House. The question was who? The obvious answer was another Land Girl and with Thea's sister Lizzie working for the Land Army in Norwich, finding one wouldn't be an issue. The problem was there wasn't space for anyone else to live long term at Rookery House – the place was already bursting at the seams. It wouldn't be fair to ask a new Land Girl to camp out in the dining room like the Waafs were currently doing. It was fine for a short stay but not as a permanent billet. While Alice made up her mind about joining the WAAF or not, or leaving for some other work, Thea needed to prepare for her departure and come up with a workable solution to replace her hard-working niece.

CHAPTER 7

14th February – Valentine's Day

There was an air of excitement in the kitchen at Rookery House tonight, Hettie thought looking around at everyone seated at the table. They'd had a full house for their evening meal with Evie here, as it was her weekend off, plus her young man Ned, along with all the others who lived here. Elspeth and Marge, the young Waafs, had eaten with them rather than at the cookhouse on the aerodrome as there was a Valentine's dance on at the village hall tonight. Most of the youngsters would be heading there in a while.

'What time do you think Father Valentine will come?' George asked. 'Will it be soon?'

Hettie turned her attention to the little boy who sat next to her, and who'd eaten all his shepherd's pie, carrots and cabbage and then polished off a helping of apple pie and custard.

'We can never tell. That's for him to decide *if* he comes here,' Hettie said. 'You just have to be patient and wait.'

'Who's Father Valentine?' Marge asked. 'I've never heard of him before.'

'We didn't know about him before we came to live at Rookery House,' Betty said. 'But he came last year, didn't he, Auntie Hettie?'

Hettie nodded. 'He did. He must have found out you were living here. Father Valentine's a bit like Father Christmas, only he doesn't come down the chimney but knocks on the door and runs away before you can answer.'

'He leaves a present for children who've been good,' Betty added, her face hopeful.

'How exciting!' Elspeth said.

'It's traditional here in Norfolk,' Thea said. 'He used to come when I was small.'

'Same with me,' Hettie added.

'Well, in that case, I hope he comes tonight then,' Marge said, smiling at Betty. 'That's if you've been good?'

Betty's eyes widened. 'I *have* been good, haven't I, Auntie Thea?'

'You have, and so have George and Emily,' Thea agreed. 'And baby Bea.' She looked around at all the children who sat at the table and Bea who was cradled in Marianne's arms.

'Should we watch out of the window for him?' Elspeth asked. 'See if we can spot him?'

'Certainly not!' Hettie said, firmly. 'If you do that and he sees you, then he won't come. Now let's get the plates and things cleared and the washing up done.'

With many hands helping to clear away, wash up and dry the dishes, it didn't take long to do the work. A short while later Hettie was sitting in a chair by the range with Emily on her lap and George and Betty standing next to her while she read them *The Tale of the Flopsy Bunnies*. The other adults sat around the kitchen table chatting.

Three sudden sharp knocks on the back door stopped the chatter and the room fell silent for a moment before George piped up, 'Is it him?' He stared at Hettie, his blue eyes wide. 'Has he been?'

'I don't know; you'd better go and look. Take Emily with you.' Hettie lowered Emily to the floor and George took hold of the little girl's hand. Together, with Betty leading the way, they headed to the back door, all the adults watching them with smiles on their faces. Reaching the door, Betty hesitated, waiting for the others to catch up, suddenly unsure about opening it and going out into the darkness.

Hettie got up and went to help. 'It's all right, just open the door and peep out, see if he's been.'

Betty nodded, grabbed hold of her brother's free hand and then slowly opened the door. Outside it was inky dark and the light from the kitchen spilled out, revealing four brown-paper parcels wrapped in string on the mat.

'He's been!' George's voice bubbled with excitement.

'See who they're for,' Hettie said. 'Betty, you go first.'

She watched as Betty let go of her brother's hand and took a tentative step out of the door to reach the spot where the parcels had been left. It was only two small footsteps outside, something the little girl wouldn't think twice about doing in daylight, but now in the darkness it was different. The coming of Father Valentine had given the night a mysterious, magical twist.

'This one's for me!' Betty grabbed a parcel and quickly retreated into the kitchen. 'George, you go with Emily. See if there's one for both of you.'

Hand in hand, the pair of them stepped outside and George was able to read Emily's name on one of the parcels, pointing it out to her so she could pick it up.

'There's one for me and that means the other must be for baby Bea,' he called back to Hettie.

'Then bring it in for her. She's too young to fetch it herself,' Hettie instructed.

He did as he was told, gathering up the last two packages and stepping back into the safety of the kitchen. Hettie closed the door behind him, blocking out the night, and the other adults who'd been watching the goings-on beckoned the children over.

'What have you got?' Thea asked.

'I don't know,' George said, standing close beside her. 'Can I open it?'

'Of course, it's got your name on it.' Thea pointed to where *George* was written in pencil on the brown paper.

Hettie watched, smiling, as each child opened their parcels. Marianne helped Emily with the knot in the string around her and Bea's packages.

'Marbles!' George exclaimed as he carefully unwrapped his parcel. 'And a bar of chocolate.' He beamed. 'Thank you, Father Valentine.'

Betty was equally delighted with a dress for her rag doll along with a bar of chocolate. Emily had a knitted teddy and some chocolate, while baby Bea had a hat and mittens.

'What wonderful presents,' Marge said. 'You're lucky to have Father Valentine come and visit here in Norfolk.'

'Aye, it's a lovely thing,' Elspeth agreed.

The back door opened and Thea's brother Reuben came in, closely followed by his faithful border collie, Bess.

'What's going on?' Reuben asked, surveying the brown

paper on the table, which had been folded up by Thea to be used again, and the lengths of string wound into a ball.

'Father Valentine's been.' Betty rushed towards him. 'He brought me these.' She held up the dress and bar of chocolate.

'That's very nice.' He patted the little girl's head.

'Did you see Father Valentine out there?' George asked.

'No, I didn't,' Reuben replied. 'No one ever sees him and if you try to spy on him coming to your house, then he won't come. We wanted to when we were children but were warned never to try to if we still wanted him to visit.'

George nodded. 'Then I'm not *ever* going to look.'

'Very wise,' Hettie agreed. She caught Reuben's eye and gave him a nod of thanks and he bowed his head in acknowledgement.

'I think it's time we left for the Valentine's dance,' Evie said, standing up. 'We'll look out and see if Father Valentine has left parcels on other doorsteps in the village.'

A short while later the kitchen was quiet and Hettie was sitting by the range knitting. Evie, Ned, Flo, Elspeth and Marge had gone to the dance, while Thea and Marianne were upstairs putting the children to bed. Hettie loved the ebb and flow of life here at Rookery House. Tonight's visit from Father Valentine had been a great success thanks to Reuben. It was a delight to see the children's eager anticipation, along with the bittersweet nervousness of having to step out into the darkness to retrieve their parcels. Hettie remembered clearly the uncertainty mixed with excitement, wondering if Father Valentine was out there in the darkness watching them get their parcels. It was a pleasure being able to share the tradition with the next generation.

With no children of her own, Hettie never had the chance

to keep the Father Valentine tradition going before she'd come to live here at Rookery House. Her decision to accept Thea's kind offer of a home had brought Hettie so much. It had opened up her world in a way she could never have expected. She'd made new friends, who'd become a family that weren't blood related but whom she'd loved getting to know. Hettie let out a sigh of happiness. She was very fortunate indeed.

CHAPTER 8

Prue could tell something was wrong as soon as she opened the door of Barker's Grocery shop. The bell jangled as normal, but this morning Grace didn't call out her usual cheery greeting from behind the long wooden counter at the rear of the shop. She was there, but had her elbows propped on the top of the counter, her head cupped in her palms as she stared at today's edition of the *Eastern Daily Press* newspaper.

'Grace?' Prue said softly as she approached her friend. Her thoughts had gone to Grace last night as she'd listened to the shocking and most unwelcome news on the wireless, in Churchill's sonorous voice, that Singapore had fallen. Grace's son Robert was in Singapore.

'I keep looking at the words, hoping they will change, that I've imagined it.' Grace put her finger on to the headline on the front of the newspaper. 'And that maybe what Churchill said last night was just a bad dream. I've been worrying enough about it happening ever since Robert went out there with his battalion. And now it has!'

Prue glanced at the headline which read **Fighting Ends At**

Singapore Unconditional Surrender Says Tokyo. It was there in bold black print. Words they'd all been dreading. Over the past week, news on the wireless and in the newspapers had been full of the latest reports about the Japanese advance towards Singapore. The island which Churchill had pledged to defend had fallen into enemy hands and, along with it, the men and women who were stationed there doing their bit to protect Singapore from invasion. Grace's son was in the 5th Battalion of the Royal Norfolk Regiment, who'd been sent out to help defend the territory against the advancing Japanese army.

'It's no use me telling you not to worry.' Prue took hold of Grace's hand, noticing the dark shadows under her friend's eyes. 'I know how you feel, how scared and helpless. I felt like that when Jack was in France and they were evacuating the troops from Dunkirk. There was nothing I could do to help him and that's hard for a mother to bear.' Jack, along with his younger brother Edwin were officially Prue's step-sons but she'd always loved them as if they were her own.

Grace's tear-filled eyes met Prue's. 'If I could, I'd go there and find my son, defend him from the enemy, bring him home...' her voice faltered. 'What am I going to do?'

'Hope. You must keep hoping, Grace. And you'll keep carrying on. It's all you can do.' Prue squeezed her friend's hand. 'I wish I could tell you different, but keeping yourself busy will help.'

'You're right, but sometimes it just feels so overwhelming,' Grace said in a shaky voice. 'I just want to scream or cry.'

'You can do that, both together, if you want. I know from experience it helps.' Prue gave a sheepish smile. 'After that, pull yourself together again and carry on.' She put her hand in her coat pocket and pulled out a piece of paper. 'Here's my shopping list. I'll pick it up on my way back from The

Mother's Day Club.' She held it out. 'I'm always here to talk to. Any time. Don't let the despair win, keep the hope going. All right?'

Grace took the list and nodded, pulling her shoulders back. 'I will and thank you. I know you understand what it feels like and I hope Robert will come through this the same as your Jack did.'

'So do I. I will be hoping alongside you. I'll see you later.'

Prue gave her friend an encouraging smile, then headed for the door thinking that if the combined power of all the hoping the women of Britain and her allies had done, and were still doing, could make a difference, then the war would have been won long ago. Unfortunately it hadn't, but it wouldn't stop them from doing it for their loved ones.

Prue wheeled the trolley with the tea urn for their mid-morning break from the kitchen into the main part of the village hall. She was glad to see that whatever was going on out in the world with the war, the members of The Mother's Day Club hadn't let it prevent them from getting on and doing their bit. The place had been a hive of activity this morning. The women were working on repairs to clothes that had been donated to their clothing depot or knitting more socks to donate to the services. A lot of the chatter had been about the fall of Singapore but now Prue wanted to turn their attention to things closer to home.

'Perfect timing!' Gloria put down the child's pinafore dress that she was re-hemming and stood up. She smoothed down the skirt of her close-fitting cherry-red dress where it had creased, then came over to collect some tea from the trolley. 'I'm parched, but maybe that's because I've been doing too much talking!' She gave a throaty chuckle as she took the cup that Prue handed her. 'Ta ducks.'

'You keep us all entertained,' Annie, another of the mothers, said as she stepped forward to collect her own tea.

'My mother always said I was never 'appier than when I 'ad an audience,' Gloria admitted. 'I suppose she was right. That's why I loved singing with a band in the dance halls so much before I was married.'

'You can get back to entertaining us in a bit,' Prue said, giving Gloria a wink as she served more tea, 'but I need to talk to you all first.'

'That sounds ominous,' Nancy said. 'Should we be worried?'

Prue smiled and shook her head. 'No, I just want to run through the plans for the allotment with you, that's all.'

Once everyone had their drinks, Prue collected her notebook and pencil and stood where they could all see her.

'Can I have your attention, please?' she called, raising her voice so it could be heard over the chatter that had started again. The women all fell silent and turned to face her.

'I won't keep you long, but I just need to talk about what we should grow on our WI allotment this year. Last year some crops were more successful than others and we want to get the highest possible yield out of our patch.' Prue glanced around at the women. 'So can we come up with a list of good, productive crops?'

'The potatoes were excellent,' Nancy said. 'Easy to grow as well.'

'Our lettuces too. Remember we even 'ad Percy Blake buying some at our stall at the summer fete after the slugs ate 'is on 'is allotment?' Gloria said.

Prue added both vegetables to her list and soon the suggestions for what to grow were coming thick and fast from the women who'd worked so hard last year, transforming an allotment overgrown with brambles, nettles and docks into a productive plot.

'At least we know what we're doing now, not like when we first started,' Gloria said. 'We achieved a lot and should be rightly proud of what we did.'

'Hear, hear,' Nancy called out, and the other women joined in. 'It taught me a lot and I love working on our allotment, seeing 'ow things grow,' she added.

'We proved Percy Blake and the other men who doubted us wrong. They won't be so quick to judge us in the future,' Prue said. 'Now we've got a list of what to grow I'll order in the seeds so we can get sowing again. Here's to another successful growing season.'

CHAPTER 9

Time had flown by since the Waafs had come to stay, Thea thought as she carried the tray holding cups of hot, milky cocoa through to the sitting room and handed them out to the three women keeping warm around the fire. Taking the last one, she settled herself in the armchair to the left of the fireplace opposite Hettie in the other armchair. Elspeth and Marge had pulled up chairs from the table and the four of them were sitting in a semi-circle around the blazing fire, which threw out a welcome heat on this cold February evening. It was just the four of them in here tonight as Marianne had gone to bed early, exhausted from lack of sleep after baby Bea had had several restless nights. Flo was having a bath and Evie was working a night shift at the hospital.

'I wish it wasn't our last evening,' Elspeth said wistfully as she cradled her cup of cocoa in her hands and stared into the flickering orange flames. 'It's been so lovely staying here with you all.'

'We've loved having you stay,' Thea said. 'I hope you'll come back and see us – you will always be welcome here.' It might have only been ten days since the Waafs had arrived, Thea thought, but they'd quickly made themselves at home and become part of their Rookery House family.

'We'll miss you,' Hettie said, her fingers working fast as she worked on the sock she was knitting to send to Marianne's husband at his POW camp in Germany.

'We'd love to come back and see you all.' Elspeth gave Thea a beaming smile. 'Wouldn't we Marge?'

Marge nodded in agreement. 'It's been wonderful living in a proper home again. Just sitting here by the fire's such a treat. I didn't realise how much I'd miss the everyday sorts of things till I joined the WAAF; you know, the simple home comforts that make a home a home.'

'It's not been very luxurious for you I'm afraid, with you having to camp out in the dining room.' Thea took a sip of her cocoa.

'Compared with sleeping in a Nissen hut it's been an absolute joy,' Elspeth reassured her.

'What are they like to live in?' Hettie asked.

'Put it this way, they're more *functional* than comfortable. I don't think comfort was high on the agenda when the RAF planned them!' Marge said, pulling a face. 'They're freezing in winter and boiling hot in summer. There's a little pot-bellied stove for heating, but unless you're right beside and virtually sitting over it, there's not much heat coming from it. So you see how we've appreciated sleeping in the dining room. Thank you for having us to stay.'

'You are both most welcome,' Hettie said. 'Do you know what time the lorry's arriving to pick you up in the morning?'

'Eleven o'clock. Hopefully we should get first pick of the beds in our new Nissen hut before the rest of the new Waafs arrive. That's something,' Elspeth said. 'It will seem strange to see the aerodrome grow to full capacity with more Waafs and

RAF on duty, and the planes will be arriving soon. Then we'll be fully operational.'

'It wasn't so long ago that the aerodrome was farmland with fields, hedges and trees,' Hettie said, a faraway look on her face. 'My sister's cottage and garden were where one of the runways is now. What had been her beautiful garden is buried under a layer of concrete. She lived there for almost forty-seven years, moved in as a young bride and was made to leave by the government.'

'That's so sad. She must have found it so hard,' Marge said.

Hettie nodded. 'She did, but she's found a new home and role at Great Plumstead Hall and is happy.'

'We don't tend to think about what was there before the aerodrome was built and how much it's changed things,' Marge said. 'It's a sobering thought so we must make all that loss and change worthwhile. Make the aerodrome work well and defend the country and help win the war!'

'Blimey, that's fighting talk Marge!' Elspeth stared at her friend, her eyebrows raised.

Marge's cheeks grew pink. 'Well, you know what I mean.'

'We do,' Hettie said. 'I hope the sacrifices made by all of us in so many ways will be worth it in the end. If we can stop that nasty Hitler then it shall be a job well done.'

'I don't think we're anywhere near a victory yet, unfortunately.' Thea shook her head. 'But we mustn't let that get us down. We need to keep going. And I meant what I said, I hope you'll both come back and visit often.'

'We will,' the two Waafs chorused.

'That's a promise,' Elspeth added with a grin.

CHAPTER 10

Prue was alone in the house, using the quiet of the Saturday afternoon to catch up on some household jobs that needed doing. Alice had gone into Norwich and Nancy had taken her daughters to do some work at the WI allotment. Victor was at work at his seed and agricultural merchants' business in Wykeham.

After an hour of cleaning, washing floors, dusting and polishing, Prue was now tackling a pile of ironing while she listened to a programme on the wireless. The Home Service was playing a selection of British Music and she was joining in, humming along to *Greensleeves* as she pressed the iron back and forth over one of Victor's shirts. Listening to music while she did a job like this, which she didn't enjoy, helped, Prue thought. It whisked her away from the task in hand, distracting her while she got the job done.

With the shirt now crease-free, Prue hung it on a hanger ready to go in the wardrobe in Victor's bedroom. Then she took another shirt from the wicker laundry basket, picked up the iron and started the process all over again.

The wireless was playing *Wistful Shepherd* when Prue heard the front door open and close, and moments later Alice appeared in the kitchen doorway, a beaming smile on her face.

'Hello Ma.'

There was something about her look of excitement, the spark in her blue eyes, that alerted Prue, making her stomach lurch. She knew her daughter well and sensed a change in her – she was different to how she had been this morning.

'Are you all right?' Prue asked putting the iron down.

'I am.' Alice pulled out a chair and sat at the kitchen table, tapping her fingers on the wooden surface for a moment before saying at last, 'I have something to tell you... I went to the recruiting centre while I was in Norwich and I've joined the WAAF!'

Prue's heart plummeted and her knees went weak. Grabbing hold of the back of a chair she steadied herself and thought for a moment before she responded. She'd known something like this was coming but it still felt much too soon. Prue wanted to say no, advise her daughter to wait, but as Alice had told her, it was far better that she volunteered so she could choose where she went. And Alice had gone and done just that.

'Speak to me, Ma. What do you think?' Alice looked uncertain.

Prue forced her mouth into a smile. 'Congratulations. I'm very proud of you but surprised too. I didn't think you'd volunteer so soon.'

'I'd made up my mind so it didn't make sense to wait any longer. The sooner I'm in the WAAF the sooner I can start doing my bit.'

'What happened at the recruitment office?' Prue pulled out a chair and sat down opposite Alice.

'I had to have a medical and I'm pleased to say I passed it.

They said I'll have to do a proficiency test during my basic training to decide what trade I'll train for. I'm not sure what I'd like to do yet, something practical and useful I think.' The words tumbled out of Alice's mouth, her enthusiasm spilling over.

'When will you go?' Prue asked, dreading the answer.

'Not sure yet, they'll send me my call-up papers along with a travel warrant and tell me then where I need to report to.' Alice's eyes sparkled with excitement. 'I can't quite believe that I'm going to be a Waaf like Patsy and the others. She told me so much about it and I know it's the right thing for me.'

'I'm sure you will make an amazing Waaf and do well in whatever job you're assigned to,' Prue said. 'You must tell Thea because she'll have to find someone to replace you.'

'I know. I wanted to tell you first and I'll go and see Thea next. I don't think she'll be that surprised because she knew I wanted to volunteer and it was only a question of time.' Alice stood up. 'I'm glad you're happy about it, Ma. I was worried about telling you. Leaving you will be the hardest bit about going. You'll be all right with me gone, won't you? I promise to write to you often.'

'Of course I will be. Now off you go and tell Thea.' Prue pasted another smile on her face and kept it there till she heard the front door close behind her daughter. Then it slipped, her shoulders slumping as she leaned her elbows on the kitchen table and put her head in her hands.

Alice was the last of Prue's children still living at home. Her presence had helped make first Jack and then Edwin's departures more bearable. Alice still being here had given Prue one child left to look out for, care for. But when she goes... Prue let out a heavy sigh. It would be the end of an era, leaving her with just Victor. She was thankful that Nancy and her girls still lived here too, so Prue wouldn't be alone with him — at least not yet.

Victor! Prue sat up straight as the question of what he would say when he found out about Alice joining the Waafs darted into her mind. He wasn't going to be pleased — and Prue would likely be in his firing line to blame for that, as well.

As they ate their evening meal, Prue felt as if she was sitting on a knife edge. The rabbit stew tasted like sawdust in her mouth and she had to force herself to eat. She was waiting for Alice to make her announcement to Victor. She'd told Prue she would do it at the table, hoping that the presence of Nancy and her daughters would help temper Victor's response a little. Waiting for it to happen was difficult as Prue kept up the pretence that everything was normal.

It was only as they were eating their dessert of bread-and-butter pudding that Prue saw Alice glance at her quickly, before turning to Victor.

'I've joined the WAAF,' Alice announced, fixing her eyes on her father. 'I signed up at the recruiting office in Norwich today.'

Prue halted the spoonful of pudding halfway to her mouth and watched as a red flush stained the neck above Victor's shirt collar and then crept upwards and suffused his face. He dropped his spoon into his bowl with a clatter and darted a glance at Prue, his icy blue eyes narrowed accusingly, his lips thinned below his moustache. Then he turned his attention to Alice, his expression mellowing slightly.

'Why?' he asked, frown lines etching his forehead.

'Because the government are going to bring in

conscription for women my age soon and I'd rather choose where I go than be sent to work in something I would hate, like a munitions factory. So I've taken matters into my own hands and decided to volunteer first. I think the WAAF will be perfect for me. I've found out a lot about it from talking to Patsy,' Alice said in a chirpy, upbeat voice.

'When are you going?' Victor asked.

'I don't know yet, but soon. They'll send me my call-up papers and a travel warrant,' Alice said. 'Then you'll have all three of your children away from home doing their bit.'

'*Two* of them!' Victor said adamantly.

Prue inwardly sighed at his continued dismissal of his youngest son, Edwin, just because he was a conscientious objector. Even though Edwin was driving ambulances, ferrying wounded soldiers somewhere in North Africa and very much doing his bit.

'A word in my study, Prudence.' Victor stood up and left the room, banging the kitchen door behind him.

'Are you really going to be a Waaf like Patsy?' Marie asked, gazing wide-eyed at Alice.

Alice nodded. 'Yes I am.'

'Well, that went down like a lead balloon,' Nancy whispered, leaning towards Prue. 'You going to his study? If you want me to come with you...'

'It's all right, I can deal with him, but thanks.' Prue gave her friend a reassuring smile, although the way her stomach was knotted she knew she wasn't feeling so assured inside.

Leaving the others in the kitchen, Prue made her way to Victor's study and pushed open the door, which he'd left ajar waiting for her. She wrinkled her nose at the smell of tobacco as she closed the door behind her and waited, looking at her husband who stood with his back to her, his hands clasped behind him as he stared out of the window.

'Victor?' she said, fighting hard to keep her voice even.

'Did you know about this?' he hissed, rounding on her, his face a mottled red.

'No, I didn't know Alice was going to sign up today. She only told me afterwards.'

'So *you* say. This is all your doing.' He jabbed his finger at her. 'Bringing that Patsy... Waaf...,' he spat out the last two words as if they burned his mouth, 'into my house, giving Alice ideas, turning her head. If anything happens to her, I will hold *you* personally responsible.'

Prue had had enough. She took a step towards Victor and a look of surprise flashed across his face, closely followed by a scowl. 'Alice was considering joining the WAAF before Patsy moved in and she's told you why she's volunteered now. I think she has done the right thing. Far better for her to have some control in how she spends the next few years or however long it will be till this war ends. She's been sensible, finding out what it's like from someone who's in the WAAF, and hasn't just been swayed by a pretty recruitment poster the way many young women are. She wants to learn, see new places, meet other people.' Prue lifted her chin and met Victor's withering gaze. 'I'm proud of my daughter for taking control and volunteering.'

Before he could respond, Prue turned on her heels and left the room, closing the door behind her.

'Everything all right?' Nancy asked getting up from where she'd been sitting at the bottom of the stairs. 'Did you tell him straight?'

Prue nodded. 'I did. And you know what, it felt good!' Her heart might have been pounding inside her while she'd faced Victor, but she was proud of the way she'd stood up to him. And what's more — she'd do it again.

CHAPTER 11

Hettie stopped turning the handle, which cranked the wooden paddles around inside the butter churn, and peered in through the clear glass side. She gave a nod of satisfaction at the sight of small golden clumps of butter which had formed as the cream from Primrose's milk was starting to separate. It didn't matter how many times she'd churned cream into butter before, she still enjoyed the process. She took hold of the handle and began to turn it again, humming a tune to herself as she worked.

It didn't take long for the clumps of butter to join into one large ball as the wooden paddles ploughed through the liquid. Hettie then unscrewed the churn lid and took it off, removing the paddles, leaving the ball of yellow butter bobbing in the pale buttermilk. She poured off the liquid into a jug to use to make pancakes later, then began the process of washing the ball of butter in cold water before mixing in a little salt. Finally, she used her wooden pats to form the butter into neat blocks. She had almost finished when the back door opened and Lizzie, Thea's youngest sister, walked in. Unlike the rest of her siblings, Thea, Prue and Reuben, Lizzie lived in Norwich and she now worked as Norfolk's County Secretary for the Land Army.

'Hello Hettie,' Lizzie greeted her warmly.

'Hello, this is a lovely surprise!' Hettie exclaimed. 'Thea's out with the WVS canteen this morning. Did she know you were coming?'

'No, she didn't.' Lizzie pulled out a chair from the table and sat down, watching as Hettie wrapped the last block of butter in greaseproof paper to be stored away in the pantry. 'It's *you* I've come to see.'

'Me?' Hettie regarded the young woman, who was looking at her with a quizzical smile on her face. 'Why? Are you all right, Lizzie? Is anything wrong?'

'I'm fine, Hettie, I promise you,' Lizzie reassured her. 'I've come here to see you in an official capacity. To ask you if you'd be willing to become a Land Army Local Representative for Great Plumstead, plus what's left of Geswick and not part of the aerodrome.'

Hettie was lost for words for a few moments after this unexpected request. She pulled out a chair and plonked herself down on it. 'I don't know what to say. What would it involve?'

'Local representatives are the Land Army's on-the-spot eyes and friendly listening ears. They're local women who look out for the Land Girls who're working on their patch and are someone who the girls can go to for friendship and help. Each Land Girl's given the name of their local representative and if they want any assistance or advice, they know they have a friendly local person they can turn to,' Lizzie explained.

'Flo's never gone to a local representative,' Hettie said.

'No, but then Flo lives here at Rookery House, where she's

happy and has people around who care for her.' Lizzie frowned. 'I'm afraid not all Land Girls are so lucky. That's why the local representative is so important. Ideally, the representative should visit each Land Girl on their patch once a month to see how they are and look out for any problems. Or I might ask you to inspect prospective employers and check the proposed living arrangements for the Land Girls. Some representatives have a party and invite their Land Girls to it. Many of the young women have never been away from home before and I see our representatives a bit like an aunt figure watching out for them, making sure they're safe, happy and being looked after properly at the farm they're working at and where they're living.'

'I see your point about needing to look after these young women. But do you think *I* could do it?' Hettie asked, her voice uncertain. 'I was a cook not a nurse or even a mother.'

Lizzie burst out laughing. 'Dear Hettie, I can think of no one better for the Land Girls to have on their side. You're warm and caring and importantly you won't take any nonsense from people. If any farmer was giving a Land Girl a hard time on your patch, I know you'd stand up for her.' She fixed her blue eyes on Hettie. 'Will you do it, please? The last local representative has had to move away to live with her daughter and now the Land Girls in this village and Geswick don't have anyone local to watch out for them.'

Hettie considered for a moment, the thought of young women like Flo needing someone to be there for them tugging at her heart. If Hettie'd had a daughter who'd gone off to live somewhere new working for the Land Army, she'd have wanted a friendly, helpful person on hand to help if needed. 'Very well, I'll give it a try.'

'Excellent!' Lizzie beamed. 'I'm on my way to visit a farmer who's applied to have two Land Girls. You could come with me, get a feel for what we look for. I have no doubt that you'll be good at this role.'

'All right, I'll come with you. I just need to put these away and wash up the churn and things.' Hettie gestured towards the wrapped pats of butter on the plate.

'Let me help.' Lizzie stood up. 'And I can tell you where this farm is while we work.'

Lizzie's Austin 7 car bounced along the rutted track leading to Yew Tree Farm on the far side of Geswick.

'Mr Chamberlain is lucky not to have lost most of his acreage to the aerodrome,' Lizzie said. 'Several of the other farms in this parish have been swallowed up by it and now acres of good land have been concreted to make runways.'

'A lot of those farms had been in the same family for generations. The government suddenly informing them their land was being requisitioned must have been hard to bear,' Hettie said. 'My sister found it bad enough losing her cottage.'

'How is Ada?' Lizzie asked, steering the car into the farmyard and bringing it to a halt in front of the farmhouse.

'Despite all that's gone on, she seems happy in her job. Being a housekeeper at Great Plumstead Hall suits Ada very well, I think. She's blossomed.' Hettie gave a soft laugh. 'To be honest, I think it might have been the best thing to have happened to her for quite a while, although I'd never dare tell her that to her face.'

'I'm glad for her, and for you. I know you were worried about her.' Lizzie touched Hettie's arm. 'Let's go and see what Mr and Mrs Chamberlain have planned for the potential Land Girls they've asked for.'

~

'This would be their bedroom,' Mrs Chamberlain said, opening the door off the landing and stepping back to allow Lizzie and Hettie to go in.

Hettie looked around the room, which was neat and clean. Two single beds stood on either side of a rag rug, there was a chest of drawers and a wardrobe, and the air smelled of lavender and beeswax polish. It was warm and welcoming.

'It's very nice,' Lizzie said, turning to Mrs Chamberlain who hovered in the doorway. 'I'm sure Land Girls would be very comfortable here.' She ticked something off on her clipboard. 'All meals would be provided?'

'Of course, all good home-cooked fare. My husband can't work on an empty stomach and the same would be true of the Land Girls,' Mrs Chamberlain replied. 'We'll look after them, don't worry.'

Lizzie caught Hettie's eye, a look of understanding passing between them.

'I'm very glad to hear that, Mrs Chamberlain. Mrs Brown here is our local representative for the area and will be keeping a close eye on your Land Girls to make sure they're happy. They'll be able to call on her for help or guidance. She's a friendly local who's there for them.'

'So we can have the Land Girls?' Mrs Chamberlain asked tentatively. 'Only we've been that stretched since our son left to join up. He could have stayed working on the farm but he wanted to go and fight.' She let out a sigh. 'We desperately need help.'

'I'm very pleased to tell you that I shall be approving your application. What you've shown me here, and what Mr Chamberlain told me earlier about what the Land Girls will be doing, shows your need and proves they will have good accommodation and be well cared for.' Lizzie gave the farmer's wife a winning smile. 'As soon as I get back to my office in Norwich, I will put the wheels in motion so your Land Girls will arrive as soon as possible.'

'Thank you.' Mrs Chamberlain returned Lizzie's smile. 'I can't tell you what a weight that is off my shoulders.' She turned to Hettie. 'I promise you, Mrs Brown, that I'll look after those young women as if they were my own family.'

'That's good to hear,' Hettie said. 'I'm always there if you or they need help.'

A short while later, Lizzie and Hettie were heading back to Rookery House.

'That was a good example of the sort of farm we're looking for,' Lizzie said. 'Mr Chamberlain had a realistic expectation of what work the Land Girls could do and his wife had sorted out a lovely room for them. I'm afraid that's not always the case and that's why we need to check carefully. You'll know what to look for if I ask you to do a prospective farm visit.'

'I've never had to do something like that before but I've got a good idea of what to do now,' Hettie said. 'I never expected this to happen to me today. There I was making butter and suddenly I have been asked to be a Land Army Local Representative!' She let out a chuckle. 'Thank you for the opportunity.'

Lizzie glanced at Hettie. 'Thank *you* for accepting. I think you'll make a first-class local rep. The Land Girls will be very lucky to have someone like you on their side.'

CHAPTER 12

Thea scooped up the last of the soiled straw with her shovel and dumped it on the pile in the wheelbarrow. Cleaning out Primrose's byre each day didn't take long and it was an important job to keep it as clean as possible. The removed straw wouldn't be wasted as it would go onto the muck heap to rot down and be used as fertiliser in the garden.

'Thea?' a voice she didn't immediately recognise called from outside.

Leaning the shovel against the wheelbarrow, Thea went to the doorway and was surprised to discover Nancy standing there. Prue's evacuee had an uncertain expression on her face, which was unusual for the sparky, confident East Ender.

'Hello Nancy. Good to see you.'

'Hettie said I could find you out 'ere.' Nancy tucked some stray hair behind her ear. 'I wondered if I could ask you something?'

Thea's first thought was that it was about Prue. Had something happened to her, was Victor being even more difficult than usual? 'Of course, is anything wrong?'

Nancy shook her head. 'No. I just wondered if you'd thought about what you were going to do after Alice leaves to become a Waaf? Have you found a replacement for 'er yet?'

'Not yet. I'm not sure what to do, but I need to do something, find someone to take on her role,' Thea said.

'Would you consider giving the job to me?' Nancy asked, her eyes meeting Thea's. 'You probably think I'm daft even thinking about it, but I've really enjoyed working at the WI allotment and love growing things. I know I ain't done anything like it before but it's opened a whole new world to me and I'd love the chance to do more.'

Thea was shocked at Nancy's proposition. 'What about your children?'

'They're at school in the day and I've 'ad a word with Gloria and she's said she'd look after them for me when they come out of school before I get 'ome, and in the 'olidays,' Nancy told her.

'I'm not...' Thea began.

'I understand if you think it's a crazy idea but maybe you could give me a trial, say three months, and see 'ow I get on? After that, if it ain't working and you're not completely satisfied with my work, you can find someone else and there'd be no 'ard feelings,' Nancy suggested. 'What do you think?'

Thea looked at the woman for a moment. Though small and wiry, Nancy was a hard worker. Prue had commented on how much time and effort she put into working at the WI allotment. Thea knew Nancy also did her share of the housework and cooking at Prue's house and was a stalwart member of The Mother's Day Club and the WI, taking part and helping in whatever was happening. She was no shirker when it came to hard work and dedication to what she believed in.

'You've caught me on the hop, to be honest, Nancy. Really

surprised me. I'm going to need to think about it,' Thea said. 'Can I let you know?'

'Of course. I didn't expect otherwise with me springing this on you. If it was me in your position, I'd 'ave to work out what was for the best.' Nancy gave Thea a hopeful smile. 'Thank you for even considering me. If you did give me a chance, I promise, 'and on 'eart, to not let you down.'

Thea nodded. 'I'll give you an answer soon. Now it's almost time for our tea break so why don't you come in and join us? Flo and Alice will be heading inside in a few minutes. You go in and tell Hettie that I'll be along shortly. I just need to take this load to the muck heap first.'

'That would be lovely, thank you,' Nancy said, then headed off to the house.

Watching her go, Thea was uncertain what she should do about Nancy's surprising offer. It was a decision that needed to be made carefully, she thought as she pushed the wheelbarrow towards the muck heap at the far end of the garden. She'd worked hard to get things going at Rookery House and having taken on Five Acres last year, there was even more work to be done. But was Nancy really the right person to replace Alice?

Reuben's railway carriage home was warm, cosy and welcoming. Thea always enjoyed popping in here some evenings for a chat with her brother. Tonight she needed his advice. Sitting down in a chair by the stove opposite Reuben, she glanced down at Bess, who lay snoozing on the rag rug, making the most of the warmth from the fire in the stove.

'What's up?' he asked, his blue eyes searching her face. 'You look like you've got a problem.'

Thea let out a laugh, causing Bess to wake up and glance at her, before resting her head on her paws again and quickly going back to sleep. 'You always could read me like a book. It's not a bad problem, more an unexpected offer.' She explained about Nancy's visit and her wanting to do a three-month trial working at Rookery House. 'What should I do?'

Reuben puffed on his pipe, then said at last. 'What were you going to do if Nancy hadn't come asking for a job?'

Thea lifted a shoulder. 'I hadn't made up my mind. Part of me was thinking we could manage because I don't have room to put up another Land Girl in the house.'

'You could have an Italian Prisoner of War. There's some started work on the farms on the estate,' Reuben said. 'It's working well. They bring them in a truck from the POW camp each morning and pick them up again in the evening.'

Thea frowned. 'I'm not sure. I don't speak any Italian for a start. Do they speak English?'

'A few can and they then tell the others what to do.'

'At least I *know* Nancy and there'd be no language difficulties with her. Prue thinks very highly of her and all the times I've seen Nancy I've never had any reason to dislike or doubt her.' Thea bit her bottom lip. 'But she's not the first person I would expect to want to work on the land.'

'Well if she says she's enjoyed what she's done at the WI allotment and she's keen on that type of work, what you do is similar, although on a bigger scale,' Reuben pointed out. 'What about her children? Do think that's going to be a problem?'

'She says not. Gloria's going to look after them when they get home from school. Although they could sometimes come back with George and Betty and play until Nancy's finished.'

'George and Betty would like that.' Reuben drew on his pipe, the tobacco glowing in the pipe bowl. 'Good for them to be with other children.'

Thea stared into the open door of the stove's firebox where the orange flames from the burning wood flickered and danced. She turned to her brother. 'I think I'll give Nancy a chance. If after three months I decide she's the not right person for the job, then I will look elsewhere for help. Alice leaving so soon hasn't given me much notice to find her replacement, so perhaps Nancy's offer is doing me a favour.'

'You'd have someone coming to work for you who's keen and wants to learn – that counts for a lot. I hope it works out for you both.' Reuben reached down and stroked Bess's head, the dog waking up to look at him and rolling over for a tummy tickle.

'So do I,' Thea said. 'I'll telephone and let Nancy know when I go back to the house. She can start as soon as Alice leaves.'

CHAPTER 13

It was the second day of March and the frost outside was mirrored by the chilly atmosphere around Victor as he walked into the kitchen for his breakfast. Prue had been expecting as much. She remained silent as she spooned some porridge from the saucepan on the stove into a bowl for him, then carried it over to his place at the end of the table.

Without a word of thanks, Victor sat down, picked up his spoon, added some stewed apple to his porridge and began to eat.

Prue got on with making some sandwiches for Alice, who was leaving this morning to become a Waaf. Providing food for her daughter's journey was something positive that she could do, Prue thought as she cut slices from the wholemeal loaf. She wished she could go with her, make sure she got to the training camp safely. But she couldn't. It was a journey Alice had to do on her own and it was time for Prue to let her go.

The sound of footsteps running down the stairs heralded

the arrival of her daughter, who burst into the kitchen positively glowing with excitement.

'Good Morning, Ma. Father,' Alice greeted them.

'Good morning.' Prue gave her daughter a welcoming smile. 'Would you like some porridge?'

'Yes, please.' Alice pulled out a chair and sat down at the table.

'Are you coming to the station to wave me off, Father?' Alice asked, looking at Victor, who'd ignored his daughter's greeting.

Prue scooped out a serving of porridge for Alice, waiting to see how Victor would respond as he'd hardly spoken to their daughter since she'd announced that she had volunteered for the WAAF.

'I'm getting the half past nine train,' Alice added.

'I'll be at work,' Victor said at last, his cold blue gaze settling briefly on Alice before he stood up, his chair's legs scraping against the tiles of the kitchen floor. Leaving half his breakfast uneaten, he gave a curt nod towards Alice and stalked out of the room. Moments later, the front door opened and closed, and he'd gone.

'No goodbye or good luck for me then!' Alice said, a look of hurt on her face.

Prue put the bowl of porridge down in front of her daughter and rested her hand on Alice's shoulder. 'I'm sorry he behaved like that.'

Alice looked up at Prue and gave a sad little smile. 'It's not your fault. If he wants to be surly and miserable, that's up to him.' She squared her shoulders, lifting her chin. 'I am not going to let it spoil things today. You'll be at the station to see me off. And Aunt Thea, Hettie and the others – plenty of people who're important to me. I never really expected Father to come.'

'No, but he should at least have said goodbye and wished you well,' Prue replied. 'I do believe he'll miss you and would rather you didn't go.'

'Then he's got a funny way of showing it,' Alice said bitterly, adding a spoonful of Rookery House honey to her porridge and stirring it in. 'You will be all right here with him when I'm gone, won't you, Ma?'

'Of course, and I won't be alone, will I? Nancy and the girls are here.' *Thank goodness*, Prue added silently, as she blinked away the tears stinging the back of her eyes and forced a smile. 'Now what would you like in your sandwiches? There's some fish paste or we can push the boat out and you could have spam?'

Prue had never been so glad to have her sister and friends around her. Standing by the train carriage, her daughter in her arms as she gave her a tight embrace, Prue wanted to beg her to stay. To not go. But of course, she would never do that. She was immensely proud of Alice and admired the young woman she had become.

'Look after yourself, won't you?' Alice said in a choked voice into her mother's ear.

Prue nodded. 'I will, I promise, and you must do the same.' With a huge effort, she loosened her hold and stepped back, looking at Alice, whose blue eyes were swimming with tears. 'Chin up and go and be the best Waaf.' She curved her lips into a smile.

With a tearful nod, Alice picked up her case and looked around at the others gathered on the platform to wave her off – Thea, Hettie, Flo, Marianne and her daughters and Nancy. 'Goodbye everyone and thank you for such a lovely send-off.'

'Take good care,' Thea said. 'And write and tell us how you're getting on.'

'All aboard,' the guard shouted from further along the platform where he was slamming carriage doors shut.

'On you get then,' Prue said. 'Safe journey.'

'Bye Ma.' Alice quickly kissed Prue's cheek and climbed on board, closing the door behind her.

As she watched her daughter find a seat by the window, Prue felt a hand slip through her arm and glanced at Thea, who'd come to stand beside her. Her sister, like Prue, was dressed in her WVS uniform.

'She'll be all right,' Thea said, squeezing Prue's arm gently.

Prue pushed down the urge to cry, keeping a smile on her face while inside her heart was breaking. Alice waved out of the window and Prue waved back along with all the others, the group of them making quite a send-off party. Moments later, the train began to move, carrying her daughter away and, as she was lost from view, Prue couldn't help the sob that escaped her.

'That's the hardest bit over,' Hettie said sympathetically, dabbing at her own eyes with a white handkerchief. 'Next time we see her, she'll be in uniform.'

Prue nodded, imagining her daughter dressed in the smart air force blue uniform like Patsy and the other Waafs. With a great effort Prue managed to get hold of her emotions again. Now wasn't the moment to give them free rein. She could do that tonight in the privacy of her bedroom. Right now everyone here would be feeling Alice's loss as she was an important part of all their lives. Prue wasn't alone there.

'Alice was pleased you all came to see her off,' Prue said. *Even when her own father wouldn't*, a voice whispered in her head. 'Thank you all for coming,' she said, pleased to hear a resilient note in her voice as she pushed all thoughts of Victor out of her mind.

'We couldn't let her go without a proper send-off,' Thea said. 'And to be here for you,' she added in a quieter voice. 'Right, we have a canteen to get on the road.'

'And we're due at The Mother's Day Club,' Hettie said, smiling at Marianne and Nancy.

The group of them headed out of the station and went their various ways. Flo on her bicycle back home to Rookery House to get on with work there, Hettie, Marianne and Nancy to open up the village hall, while Prue and Thea climbed into the WVS canteen which Thea had parked by the station after going into Wykeham earlier to pick it up.

Prue sat silently staring out of the window as they drove along, noticing a group of lorries heading towards RAF Great Plumstead. Life was going on as normal, or as normal as it had been since the start of the war, despite her daughter's departure.

'You're very quiet,' Thea said. 'Are you all right?'

'Not really, but I have to get on with things, don't I?' Prue said in a flat voice. 'I hate seeing my children off and with Alice being the last to go...'

Thea reached out and touched Prue's arm. 'I understand. But she wouldn't want you to be miserable.'

Prue nodded. 'It's just...'

'What?'

'It feels as if part of me went with her, like I've lost a limb. I know that sounds ridiculous.'

'Not at all.' Thea gave her a sideways glance. 'She's your daughter. You've been together since before she was born so it

66

will take some adjusting to, but you'll get there.' She brought the canteen to a stop at a junction and, after checking it was clear, turned right. 'The best thing to do is keep yourself busy — and that's something you're an expert at!'

Prue's mind went over the various things that kept her busy and would be more important than ever now. The Mother's Day Club, the WI and working for the WVS either here in the canteen or doing other tasks like salvage collections, not forgetting the WI's allotment. She did have plenty to keep her occupied and away from home, because home was where she would miss Alice the most. She took a deep breath and raised her chin. 'You're right, Thea. Keeping busy is my way to get through this. And with the war still on, there's never a shortage of things that need doing.'

CHAPTER 14

'Is that everything?' Hettie looked over the things laid out on the dining room table.

Marianne checked her list. 'I think so. I've ticked each item off as we put it out. Let's hope when they're all added together and wrapped in paper and string they don't weigh over ten pounds. The leaflet makes it clear that's the maximum weight limit.' She gestured towards the pamphlet she'd had from the Red Cross, who oversaw sending the next-of-kin parcels to POWs.

'If it does then we'll have to prioritise and save something for next time. How soon will that be?'

'In another three months! That's the rule. We can only send Alex one of these parcels four times a year. So we'll have to fit as much as we can in,' Marianne said, her expression resolute. 'I'd really like him to get *all* of these things. They'll help make his life in the camp a little easier.'

Hettie was glad to be helping her friend prepare the parcel to send to her husband at his POW camp in Germany. They'd spent the past few weeks buying or making things he'd asked for in his letters. Hettie had knitted him socks, gloves and a balaclava while Marianne had been allowed extra clothing coupons to buy him some striped pyjamas. Now that Emily and baby Bea were both having an afternoon nap it was the perfect time to put the parcel together.

Hettie put a hand on her friend's arm for a moment. 'Let's find out if it can all go in. Shall we start by weighing everything together, before we do any wrapping?'

'Good idea,' Marianne agreed.

Hettie had brought her kitchen scales into the dining room along with a ten-pound metal weight to measure the items against. Together they piled things onto the empty pan on one side of the scales, first the pyjamas, some underwear, the knitted garments, bootlaces, two towels and a flannel, then soap, some pencils, a housewife sewing kit with needles and threads for mending clothes, dentifrice powder and a toothbrush, shaving soap and a safety razor and blades, some shoe polish and a shoe brush.

Together they watched anxiously as the scales moved – the side with the things to send going down, while the ten-pound weight slowly began to rise.

'There's just the paper and string to add,' Marianne said.

Hettie watched as Marianne placed the folded sheet of brown parcel paper and length of string on top. The weighted side of the scales was still lowest, but only by a little.

'It's just under ten pounds!' Marianne declared, a look of relief on her face.

'We could add something else. How about a book?' Hettie suggested.

Marianne shook her head. 'No, books aren't allowed. The Red Cross sends them separately.'

'Or some candles?'

'They're not on the list of allowed items either.'

'We could put just one in. How would they know what's inside the parcel once it's been wrapped up?' Hettie asked.

'Because each parcel is opened at the next-of-kin parcel centre and the contents checked before it's sent off. Anything that's not allowed will be taken out,' Marianne said. 'There's no point in sending anything that's not on the permitted list. Even if we'd like to send it to Alex and it would be useful to him.' She gave a soft sigh. 'Apparently the list is so strict to protect the prisoners by keeping to what the Germans will allow to be sent. I don't want to put Alex in any danger so we must stick to the list. At least all this can go in the parcel.'

'Let's get it wrapped up and you can take it down to the post office this afternoon when the children wake up.' Hettie took hold of the brown paper and spread it out on the table and together they carefully piled the items from the scales in the middle of it, fitting everything in neatly. Then they wrapped the paper around it, making neat folds and tucks of the ends, before encircling the entire parcel with string, from opposite side to opposite side.

'Hold your finger where the strings cross to keep it tight,' Hettie instructed.

Marianne did as she was asked, keeping the string in place as Hettie tied a knot, quickly slipping her finger out as it tightened. Finishing it with a secure double knotted bow, the parcel was ready to send.

'All done,' Hettie said. 'Now we can start planning for the next one. We've got three months to make clothes or buy whatever Alex needs. The more time the better with rationing going on. It's not so easy to get our hands on things these days.'

'I thought I could make him some shirts to send next time,' Marianne said. 'They are most definitely on the allowed list!'

The sound of a cry came from upstairs. Bea was awake and, with all that noise, Emily soon would be too.

'We're finished just in time!' Marianne said. 'Thank you for your help, Hettie. I appreciate it and I know Alex will be grateful for the socks and other things you knitted him.'

'I'm glad to help and I'll keep knitting all I can. You see to the girls and I'll clear up here,' Hettie said.

After Marianne had gone upstairs, Hettie rolled up the leftover string to be reused, thinking how bittersweet sending Alex a parcel felt. On the one hand, it was good that Marianne could do this for her husband providing him with things he needed, but on the other it was sadly her only way of contacting him other than letters. Like so many wives separated from their husbands by war, Marianne had to make the best of the situation. At least she was not alone – Hettie, along with all the others living out the war at Rookery House, would carry on doing whatever they could to help her.

CHAPTER 15

Thea watched as Flopsy, the female rabbit, tucked into the hay, her nose and whiskers twitching as she ate.

'You fill yourself up, you've got babies to feed now,' Thea said softy as she secured the run attached to the rabbit's hutch where she'd put a large pile of feed for Flopsy. Along with the hay, there were fresh cabbage leaves, dandelion leaves and other plants that Thea had foraged around the grounds of Rookery House.

Thea resisted the urge to have a peek inside the hutch where Flopsy's new babies were safely snuggled in a warm nest made of hay and lined with fur the mother rabbit had pulled from her belly. It wasn't a good idea to disturb the newborns often and they'd already been peeped at this morning by George and Betty before they went to school, along with Thea. They'd all been eager to see if Flopsy had given birth during the night. Thea wasn't sure how many babies there were yet. They would have to wait a while to find out.

With a final inspection of Flopsy and then the buck rabbit, Benjamin, who was tucking into his food in the neighbouring run, Thea headed off to the greenhouse. As she walked through the garden, the sound of engines approaching overhead made her look up to see one of the recently arrived planes from RAF Great Plumstead. Since they'd flown in a few days ago, they had become a regular sight in the skies above the village. Their engines sounded different to those of enemy planes, so at least Thea wasn't put on edge when they passed over.

Approaching the greenhouse, she could see Flo and Nancy inside, busy at work. She'd given them the task of sowing broad bean, leek and tomato seeds. Flo would be able to keep an eye on Nancy and help her out if needed. Although since Nancy had started her new job here yesterday, Thea had had no cause for concern over the woman's work. If Nancy didn't know something, or wasn't sure, she always asked and was eager to do the right thing. She seemed to be enjoying herself too.

'Sleeping in the underground ain't the most comfortable way to spend the night but it was better than staying in the 'ouse,' Nancy was saying to Flo as Thea opened the greenhouse door and stepped inside.

She was met by the rich earthy smell of soil that she loved, as she associated it with growing things and happy days spent outside in the garden.

Nancy turned to Thea and gave her a welcoming smile. 'We're getting on nicely with the sowing.' She gestured at the neatly labelled plant pots which had already been done.

Thea returned the smile. 'It looks like good work. It's much warmer in here than outside. The sunshine's warming it up nicely which will help the seeds grow.'

'Nancy was just telling me about the Blitz,' Flo said. 'It was a lot worse than what we experienced in Manchester. London was attacked night after night. Our two-night Christmas Blitz was bad enough but to think of the planes coming back again and again...,' her voice trailed off.

'Your Blitz might 'ave been short but it still cost you dear,' Nancy said, her voice gentle as she put a hand on Flo's arm.

Flo nodded, biting her bottom lip. 'Too many people have lost family in bombings,' she said at last. 'But it brought me to Rookery House and I do love being here.' She glanced at Thea, their eyes meeting.

'And we're glad you came.' Thea's heart ached for the young woman who'd lost her parents, sister and brother in Manchester's Christmas Blitz in 1940. It wasn't something Flo spoke of much, and when she'd first come to live and work here she'd kept it private. Since then, she had revealed her past loss and was slowly coming to terms with it, but she still missed her family dearly. Perhaps having Nancy come to work here would help Flo to talk about it more.

'Having my 'ouse bombed brought me 'ere too,' Nancy said. 'Look at me now, someone who'd never grown a thing in 'er life and 'ere I am sowing seeds!' She let out a laugh. 'Who'd 'ave believed it!'

'The war has changed many things for us all,' Thea said. She fell silent for a moment, thinking of some of the tricky situations they'd been through since the start of the war, but quickly snapped herself back to the present. 'Right, I'm going to take the veg down to Barker's so I'll see you in a bit.'

Leaving them in the warmth of the greenhouse, Thea collected the basket of freshly harvested leeks, Brussel sprouts and winter spinach that she'd left ready by the shed and fastened it onto the back of her bicycle. A quick trip into the village to deliver these and then she'd come back and get on with the next job. There was never a shortage of things that needed doing here, but she loved it, she thought as she climbed onto her bike and pushed off, cycling around to the front gate and on to the road. Life at Rookery House was a busy one, but she wouldn't swap it for anything.

CHAPTER 16

It was Saturday afternoon and Prue was making her way back home from the village hall. She and some women from The Mother's Day Club had spent the past few hours having a sort through and stock-take of the clothing depot, which was stored in one of the hall's large walk-in cupboards. This morning, when the hall wasn't being used by the regular Mother's Day Club meetings, had been a good time to do it as they'd needed plenty of space to work.

The stock-take had shown that more clothing was badly needed as they were running low on many things. With lots more children living in the village now, each of them growing bigger and frequently requiring larger clothes, they went through outfits much faster than adults. Prue would have to try to source more clothes from somewhere or the material to make some. It was another thing to add to her long list of things to be done.

'You look miles away!'

The man's voice caught Prue by surprise. She turned

around to see their village postman walking towards her carrying a parcel.

'I was just on my way to your house to deliver this.' He held out the parcel to her.

Prue took it and checked the address written on the brown paper, instantly recognising the writing – it was from Alice. It must be her clothes. She'd been told to take brown paper and string to send her civilian clothing home once she'd swapped it for her new uniform. Prue managed a smile, while inside she felt like crying. 'Thank you.'

The postman touched the rim of his peak cap and left to continue with his round.

Prue tucked the parcel under her arm and headed home. A feeling of urgency propelled her on so she could open it and have some contact with Alice, no matter how fleeting and distant. Common sense told her that Alice wasn't back. She wasn't in her clothes. But Prue missed her so much she was desperate to see the things her daughter had been wearing the last time she saw her.

Reaching the house, she hurried indoors, shrugged off her coat and draped it on the newel post at the bottom of the stairs rather than hanging it on the stand as she usually would, then went into the kitchen. She placed the parcel on the table and paused, staring at it, wanting to savour the anticipation but at the same time in a hurry to tear off the paper. But she couldn't do that. The paper needed to be saved to use again.

Slowly and carefully Prue undid the knot of the string, removed it from the parcel and then unwrapped the paper. She gasped as she saw Alice's clothes and her shoes in a neat pile. Gently placing the shoes to one side, she picked up the soft wool jumper and held it to her cheek, breathing in the lingering scent her daughter wore. Prue closed her eyes and let herself imagine for a moment that Alice was here, back home and everything was as it had been.

The sound of the front door opening and voices – Marie and Joan's, followed by Nancy's as she reminded them to hang up their coats – brought Prue back to the present. They'd all been out working at the WI allotment. She inhaled a last breath of Alice's scent and quickly folded the jumper, replacing it on the pile of other clothes. Prue was winding the string around her fingers when Nancy and the girls came into the kitchen.

'What's that…?' Nancy asked, seeing the parcel, then her voice tailed off as realisation dawned. 'Go upstairs and wash your 'ands thoroughly, girls. Get the soil out from under your fingernails.' She ushered her daughters out of the kitchen and shut the door behind them. 'You look gutted if you don't mind me saying so.' Nancy strode across the room and put her arm around Prue. 'Seeing Alice's clothes returned 'as 'it you 'ard, ain't it?'

Prue nodded, her eyes filling with tears. 'I'm being silly. It's just her clothes and I knew she'd be sending them back. But…' she waved her hand in air. 'I can smell her perfume on them. It makes me miss her even more!'

'I understand. But part of being a parent is 'aving to let your children fly the nest. Easy for me to say I know when my two are just upstairs. But one day it'll be their turn to go and I know I'll feel lost,' Nancy admitted. 'Come on, let's make something to eat. It will 'elp you feel better.'

After they'd all eaten, and the girls had gone up to play in their room, Prue and Nancy sat at the kitchen table having a cup of tea. Prue was feeling brighter than before. The vegetable soup and bread had filled her up after the morning's work and the lively chatter of Marie and Joan had cheered her. Their enthusiasm about working at the allotment with Nancy was heartening.

'Can I ask you something?' Nancy stirred some milk into her freshly poured cup of tea.

'Of course.'

'I've been wondering what you were planning to do now that Alice is gone?' Nancy looked directly at Prue. 'You once told me that the reason you were still married to Victor is that you were biding your time until Alice left. Then you'd be making changes. Have you decided what to do yet?'

Prue was about to take a sip of tea but instead put her cup down, surprised at Nancy's direct question. It was true, though; she had told her friend that when she'd questioned why Prue was married to a man like Victor. Nancy had often witnessed how unpleasant he was, how dismissively he treated Prue, their marriage clearly one in name only, with no affection or care. Now Alice had left, Victor barely spoke to Prue, keeping his communication with her to a minimum. There was no question that Prue's marriage was an empty shell, and a cracked and crumbling one at that.

'Prue?' Nancy's voice interrupted her thoughts.

'I did say that... and now Alice has gone, and I need to decide what to do.' Prue let out a sigh, her fingers slowly turning her cup around in her hands, while her mind raced through different scenarios. 'But things aren't so simple. If I tell Victor I want a divorce, then I know I'd lose my home. I'd have to leave here, and if I go, then I'm afraid you and the girls would have to leave too. I can't see Victor allowing you to stay on. I couldn't do that to you all.'

Nancy threw up her hands and let out a bark of laughter. 'We've coped with 'itler's planes bombing us out. We could cope with Victor moving us on.' She leaned forwards in her seat, her eyes fixed on Prue's. 'Please, Prue, don't let worrying about us stop you from escaping… from being free and 'appy. Victor has 'eld sway over you for far too long. It's time for you to get away from 'im and 'is measly ways. You deserve much, much better than being married to 'im.'

Prue bit her bottom lip, tears stinging the backs of her eyes. Hearing Nancy say those words, voicing the prospect of Prue's freedom, made for a heady mix of thoughts and feelings swirling through her. Yes, she did want to be free, to not have to consider Victor's reactions to things. To not feel like she was treading on eggshells when he was around. Or have to put up with his rude unpleasantness anymore. Whatever she decided, Prue knew she must make careful preparations to protect and provide for herself.

'I need to think about it before I decide how to proceed.' Prue lifted her chin. 'You're right, Nancy. I shouldn't stay with someone like Victor, but I must be careful how I go about it. He's not a man to be fooled with. Changes are coming, just give me time to work things out and do the best I can for all of us.'

Nancy nodded. 'All right, fair enough. Just remember I'll be beside you all the way if you want me.'

Prue gave her friend a grateful smile. Having someone like Nancy in her corner was a huge help. But ultimately it was up to Prue to decide if she was brave enough to cut loose from her marriage, sham though it was.

CHAPTER 17

'Those baby bunnies are such dear wee things,' Elspeth said, sitting down at the kitchen table alongside George who'd been eager to show the Waafs the latest arrivals at Rookery House.

'They are, but they're not pets.' Thea placed some cups and small plates on the table.

'We often have to remind ourselves of that because they are so lovely,' Hettie said, opening the round tin she'd fetched from the pantry, revealing a golden, cinnamon-scented freshly baked apple cake. 'But we can't keep them all.'

'My father's started keeping rabbits for meat back at home in Kenilworth,' Marge said. 'Just as well I'm not there or I might get too fond of them.'

Hettie gave the Waaf an understanding smile. The two young women had bicycled over from the aerodrome on their Sunday afternoon off for a visit. Hettie was pleased to see them both as she missed them now they'd moved out. 'Who'd like a slice of cake?'

'Yes please,' George and Betty piped up in unison.

'And me, please,' Elspeth said with a grin. 'The cooks in the cookhouse on the aerodrome could certainly do with some lessons from you, Hettie.'

'Sometimes it's hard to work out what exactly the food's supposed to be,' Marge added. 'I thought it was a stew the other day and apparently it was a shepherd's pie! It didn't look like any shepherd's pie I'd ever had before. I don't know where the mashed potato topping had gone – I didn't get any in my serving.'

'Count yourself lucky because the potato I got was full of grey lumps,' Elspeth said with a shake of her head.

Once they'd all been served and had a slice of cake on a plate in front of them and a cup of tea, or a glass of milk for the children, Hettie sat down in her usual seat at the end of the table. 'How are things on the aerodrome? Are you settled into your new accommodation?'

Marge nodded as her mouth was full of cake. 'Yes, we're getting used to it,' she said after swallowing. 'We're sharing the hut with a good group of girls. And our work is busier than ever with the aerodrome about to become operational.'

'We've seen the planes flying around a lot,' Thea said.

'Where will they fly to?' George asked.

'I don't know,' Elspeth said. 'They keep information like that top secret and only tell those who need to know.' She winked at the little boy.

'Have you heard from Alice?' Marge asked.

'We had a letter the other day and she seems to be getting on all right. Still doing her basic training,' Thea said.

'That means lots of marching and being bossed around then.' Elspeth rolled her eyes. 'I remember it well and was glad to get through those first weeks. They're the toughest.'

'We all miss her,' Hettie said. 'We saw Alice nearly every day after she started working here and we got used to her being about the place.'

'I'm sure she'll enjoy herself and get to go to new places and meet lots of people. That's one of the things I love about being in the WAAF,' Elspeth said. 'If I hadn't joined up then I'd still be living on the farm at home and wouldn't have travelled beyond Scotland. I wouldn't have met any of you!'

'I felt the same when I volunteered to drive ambulances in the Great War,' Thea said. 'It took me miles away from home and I met my best friend Violet there. It wasn't easy but I'm glad I did it.'

'I'm going to be a Waaf when I grow up,' Betty declared.

Hettie reached over and put her hand on the little girl's arm. 'I hope this war will long be over by the time you're old enough to join up.'

The other adults nodded in agreement, their eyes meeting at Betty's poignant declaration.

'Maybe I'll be a nurse like Evie instead,' Betty said looking thoughtful. 'They always need nurses, don't they?'

'They certainly do,' Hettie agreed. 'And I think you'd make a good nurse.'

Taking a sip of her tea, Hettie listened as the others chatted, the conversation turning to other topics. She sometimes despaired at how much this war was affecting children like George and Betty. It wasn't just that they'd had to move from their homes in London to live here – that was enough of an upheaval. It was also how they absorbed other things they saw. How it affected the way they thought and what they regarded as normal life. Wartime was anything but normal. Yet for these children, and thousands like them, this was all they'd known or could remember, having been too young to recall life in peacetime. It made occasions like this, sharing friendship and good cheer, even more important for all of them – the children, these young Waafs and everyone here at Rookery House.

CHAPTER 18

'It was lovely having Elspeth and Marge visiting yesterday afternoon. They feel like part of our Rookery House family now, even though they didn't live with us for that long,' Thea said as she drove the WVS canteen along a lane whose banks were dotted with butter yellow aconites and white snowdrops. She glanced at Prue, who was sitting silently staring out of the front window. 'Prue? Are you all right? You're very quiet this morning.'

'Sorry.' Prue turned to face Thea. 'What were you saying?'

'I asked if you're all right, only you've not said a lot this morning and obviously haven't been listening to me either!'

Prue shook her head. 'I'm not all right, to be honest. I hardly slept last night because I had so much going round and round in my mind. So many questions and not enough answers.'

Thea checked her wing mirror and then pulled the canteen over into a gateway and switched off the engine. 'Tell me about it.'

'The parcel with Alice's clothes in arrived on Saturday and

it, well... it made me miss her all the more. And then Nancy came home and asked me what I was going to do now. When was I planning to end things with Victor like I said I would once Alice left?' Prue let out a heavy sigh, looking down at her hands, which were clasped in her lap. 'Only it's not as simple as that because I know he'll throw me out along with Nancy and her daughters too. They've already lost one home.'

'Is that all that's stopping you from leaving him? Not having a home to go to?' Thea probed.

Prue nodded. 'Mostly.'

'Well, you needn't worry about that because you, Nancy and the girls can *all* come and live at Rookery House.'

'But you haven't got any space!' Prue looked up at Thea.

'Well you could always share my room and Nancy and the girls could have the dining room. We used to share a bedroom as children so we've done it before and could do it again.' Thea grabbed hold of Prue's hand. 'Honestly, Prue, *please* don't let fear of having nowhere to go stop you from gaining your freedom.'

Prue blinked rapidly. 'Thank you, that's very kind of you. And it really helps, if you truly mean what you say. It wouldn't be for ever but it would get us all out of there and away from Victor.'

'I do mean it! So when are you coming to stay, then?' Thea asked.

'I'm not sure. I'll need to prepare first. I know that as soon as I tell Victor I want a divorce, then he'll make things extremely difficult for me. Cut off money, make me out to be the home wrecker, a marriage breaker.' She huffed. 'Even though he's the adulterous one!'

'You can use the fact that he's having an affair to get him to comply with a divorce, can't you?' Thea asked.

'Knowing Victor, I very much doubt it.' Prue frowned. 'He

would somehow do his best to wriggle out of it and get what he wants. I need to be wary.'

Thea opened her mouth to speak but closed it again, knowing she needed to rein herself in and think before she spoke because Prue was in a delicate frame of mind and tricky situation. Thea had never and would never allow a man to dominate and rule her life the way her sister had. But she knew the reason why Prue had gone into such a marriage with a man like Victor. It was hard to watch over the years, and Thea had been relieved to see the small steps Prue had taken since the start of the war to lessen the hold Victor had over her. The necessities of wartime had made it easier for her sister to make changes in their home. However, there was still a good way to go yet and Victor still dominated Prue's life.

After taking a steadying breath Thea said, 'I understand. But don't leave it too long, will you? You've already given enough years to that man. It's time for you to escape and not be controlled by him anymore.'

'I wish I was more like you. You wouldn't dither like this,' Prue said in a small voice.

'I would never have married him in the first place and he wouldn't have married me either. We've never got along.' Thea's eyes met her sister's. 'Remember, I'm here for you any time, day or night, and Rookery House is ready for you all. Just say the word.'

Prue squeezed Thea's hand. 'Thank you. I will get there, I *will* be free. I've promised myself that. I need a little time, that's all.'

Thea nodded. 'I'll try to be patient. I just want you to be happy.'

Prue smiled a sad smile. 'I know. And I am most of the time. There are many wonderful things in my life that give me great joy. I try to focus on that. Now, are we going to get this canteen to the troops this morning or not?'

Thea knew her sister well enough to know that she wouldn't get any more out of Prue about leaving Victor for the moment. Starting the engine, Thea checked her wing mirror and pulled out onto the road, promising herself that she would be keeping a close eye on Prue over the next few weeks, months, or however long it took for her sister to break free of the man who'd been like a thorn in her side for years. Thea would be there waiting, ready to help and support Prue in every way she could.

CHAPTER 19

Hettie pedalled along the lane, enjoying the early April day. The sun was gently warming the countryside and plants were responding with a spurt of growth or by sending up their spring flowers to paint the hedgerows. The primroses were putting on a good display this year, Hettie thought, admiring a particularly large patch of delicate pale-yellow flowers nestling in a sheltered hollow on one bank of the road. The birds were singing, eager to get their nest building and raising young underway. The whole feeling of the world awakening anew after the colder winter months filled Hettie with joy.

She was out on a mission this afternoon as a local Land Army Representative. Lizzie had given her the job of going to a farm which had recently applied to have a Land Girl and Hettie's task was to assess the accommodation that would be provided. It was on the far side of Great Plumstead, just into the next parish.

Reaching the turning leading to Crossways Farm, Hettie turned her bicycle off the road and tutted at the state of the track down to the farmhouse. It was riddled with dips and bumps which, if she wasn't careful, could jar her off her bicycle. Riding slowly and taking care to steer a safe path through the maze of potholes, Hettie thought that first impressions of the farm weren't favourable.

Her arrival was greeted by a dog rushing out from one of the barns and barking loudly at her, before a loud, gruff voice called out 'Roy, come here,' and the dog retreated into the barn from which a man was now emerging out of the shadows, shielding his eyes against the brightness of the day.

'Good afternoon,' Hettie called, dismounting and leaning her bicycle against the barn wall. 'I'm the Land Army's Local Representative for this area and have come to inspect the lodgings you'd provide for a potential Land Girl. Are you Mr Southgate?' Hettie asked, having already been briefed by Lizzie on the telephone.

'That's right.' The man took off his peak cap and wiped his forehead with the arm of his jumper before replacing his hat. 'What do you want to know?'

'I'd like to see the Land Girl's room – where she'd be sleeping.'

'It's this way.' Rather than leading her towards the farmhouse, Mr Southgate crossed the farmyard to another barn and went in.

Hettie followed him, her eyes taking a moment to adjust to the gloom inside the barn.

'Up there.' Mr Southgate pointed to a rickety flight of wooden stairs that led to an upper storey. 'Take a look.'

Thinking that this wasn't boding well, Hettie reserved judgement and carefully climbed the stairs, taking care to hold on to the wall and the stair rail which wobbled alarmingly in her hand. The sight that greeted her as she rose just high enough to see the upper floor filled her with anger. The floorboards were thick with dust and dead flies. Cobwebs festooned the overhead beams and she could see daylight through several gaps in the tiles overhead.

'We'll put a camp bed up there. Should be nice and cosy,' Mr Southgate called up.

His warped interpretation of cosy fanned the flames of Hettie's anger, but she waited until she'd safely descended the staircase before she told him exactly what she thought. Compared with what she had seen on offer at Yew Tree Farm when she'd visited it with Lizzie, six weeks or so ago, this place was an utter disgrace.

'I have to say that *your* interpretation of cosy is a whole world away from *mine!*' Hettie said, puffing up her chest and fixing her eyes on Mr Southgate. 'How do you plan to heat this…' she waved her hand upwards, 'bedroom?'

'There'll be blankets on the bed.'

'And where would the Land Girl wash?'

'There's a cold tap out in the yard. Same as I use to fill up the buckets for the pig's water trough.'

'And you *really* think this is suitable accommodation for a hard-working Land Girl, do you?' Hettie asked in a sharp voice. 'Would *you* want to sleep up there?'

'Well it's…' Mr Southgate looked down at his boots.

'If that's all you have to offer, then I'll be recommending that the Land Army turn down your application. The accommodation you're offering is not fit for purpose. It's filthy, cold, there are holes in the roof…' Hettie counted out the issues on her fingers, 'and washing facilities are inadequate.' Hettie turned to go.

'Wait! I suppose she *could* have a room in the house,' the farmer said, grudgingly.

Hettie tapped her foot on the ground. 'Let me see it then.'

Looking shame-faced, Mr Southgate led the way to the farmhouse and in through the kitchen door. 'This is my wife,' he said indicating the woman who was peeling potatoes at the sink. 'The barn's not good enough for a Land Girl,' Mr Southgate told his wife. 'So I've said there's a room in the house.'

Mrs Southgate let out a sigh, wiping her hands on a tea towel. 'I *told* you it wasn't fit. Now go and get on with your work and I'll show...'

'Mrs Brown,' Hettie said.

'Mrs Brown, the bedroom.' She waited until her husband had left, watching him through the window and shaking her head. 'I told him, but he wouldn't have it. Come on, let me show you the room.'

Hettie followed Mrs Southgate upstairs to a small but pleasant bedroom, with a single bed and chest of drawers. It was clean and tidy and a world away from the barn offering.

'Why on earth did Mr Southgate want to put a Land Girl in a barn instead of in here?' Hettie asked, turning to the farmer's wife.

'He's not keen on strangers and having one living in the house.' She tutted. 'But if he wants help on the farm, then he's going to have to put up with it. To be honest, I'd be glad of someone else living here, some company other than my husband. He's not one for talking much.'

'I'll tell you straight that this room is perfectly acceptable, but the barn is *not*,' Hettie said firmly. 'If you're prepared for the Land Girl to sleep in here, then I will inform the Land Army office in Norwich that I approve your accommodation.'

'You have my word that this will be her bedroom,' Mrs Southgate assured her.

'Fair enough, but I'll be checking on her to make sure all is well. It's part of my role.'

'I wouldn't want any daughter of mine to go and work at a farm and sleep in a barn so I promise you she'll be well looked after. My husband's just going to have to get used to things changing around here.' Mrs Southgate put her hand on her hip. 'He can either like it or lump it! I'm looking forward to having a Land Girl come here. And you're welcome to come back anytime and check on her. Now have you got time for a cup of tea before you go?'

'I do, thank you.'

As Hettie followed the farmer's wife downstairs to the kitchen, she was relieved that the Land Girl who'd be sent here would have a decent room and hoped that she'd get on well with both Mr and Mrs Southgate. If not, Hettie would be back to sort things out.

CHAPTER 20

Glancing up from a last-minute check of her list, Prue saw that the village hall was filling up for tonight's Women's Institute meeting. Some familiar air force blue caught her eye, and she was delighted to see that Patsy and three other Waafs had just arrived. Prue had mentioned the WI meetings to the young woman and had encouraged her to come along and bring any other interested colleagues with her. She knew Hettie had done the same with the two Waafs who had stayed at Rookery House.

Leaving her list on the table at the front, Prue made her way to the back of the hall, greeting other members as she went.

'Hello Patsy, I'm so glad you could come,' Prue welcomed the Waaf and her friends with a warm smile. 'We've got an interesting talk and demonstration tonight about make-up and hairdressing and how to get the most out of what's available to us now.'

'I could do with some help with that.' Patsy patted her hair, which was pinned up above her collar as per the WAAF regulations. 'Can I have a word with you, Prue? Only I've got something to ask you, well the whole village WI really.'

Prue nodded. 'Of course.'

'Elspeth, Marge!' A delighted voice called across the hall and Prue looked around to see Hettie heading towards them, a beaming smile on her face.

'Hettie, can you see to our guests, make sure they're settled in a good seat?' Prue asked. 'Patsy needs to speak to me for a moment.'

'I'd be happy to,' Hettie replied, then turned her attention to the other Waafs, giving the two whom she knew a warm hug and shaking the hand of the other new Waaf.

Leaving Hettie to look after the other young women, Prue steered Patsy towards the front of the hall near the table where the WI committee sat during meetings and where it was quieter.

'What do you want to ask me? Is everything all right at the aerodrome for you?'

'Everything's fine. We're all settled in now and as comfortable as we can be in a Nissen hut. I have a request on behalf of the men of RAF Great Plumstead — and their hole-riddled socks! With the Group Captain's permission, I've come to ask the WI if they'd help by darning the men's socks? The men have tried themselves and made a real hash of it.' She giggled. 'They even asked us Waafs to do it for them but we've already got enough to do keeping our own stockings in good order. So we wondered if the WI could help?'

'I'm sure we can. Our members have years of experience and would make a far better job of it than the men on your aerodrome. I'll ask for volunteers.'

'Thank you,' Patsy said. 'They'll really appreciate it.'

Prue glanced at her watch. 'It's almost time to start the

meeting. Go and sit yourself down. Your friends have saved you a seat and I hope you enjoy tonight.'

Sitting herself at the table, Prue quickly added Patsy's sock-darning request to her list. It was yet another thing she'd be asking the members to help with but she didn't doubt they would be willing to assist.

Judging by the volume and enthusiasm of the chatter at the interval, the first half of the meeting had been well received by the WI members and guests. Tonight's invited speaker's talk and demonstration had been packed with information, along with plenty of tips and tricks for make-up and hairdressing. There'd been no shortage of willing volunteers to help demonstrate the techniques. Now it was time for Prue to call the women back to their seats and get down to the business part of the meeting.

'Can you all take your seats again, please?' Prue called out from the front of the hall.

It didn't take long for the women to return empty cups to the table of tea things and settle back into their places once more.

'Before we begin our games and singing, I have several important things to go through with you and which I hope you'll help with.' Prue paused, looking around at the women who sat watching her. 'I'm sure many of you will have heard about Lord Woolton's announcement yesterday concerning the Rural Pie Scheme.' Prue was glad to see plenty of heads nodding in the audience. 'If you have you'll know he's appealed to organisations like us and the WVS to help distribute food to workers in the countryside who don't have access to ration-free foods like those who work in factories with canteens, or who can buy a meal in a British Restaurant.

There aren't many of those around here!' The women laughed. 'We need volunteers to distribute food to the workers. It would be pies but also sandwiches and snacks. There's plenty to organise. Firstly, I need to find a baker to make the pies. But without people willing to take food to the workers, the scheme won't be able to run. Please raise your hand if you'd like to volunteer to help get the food out to those who need it either by bicycling or walking around. I also need help to run a stall here in the village selling the food.'

'I could use my pram to make deliveries,' Gloria called out.

'So could we,' added several other mothers who had prams for their children.

'Who's willing to 'elp out?' Gloria called, sticking her hand in the air.

One by one, hands went up across the hall. Not everyone was willing or able, but Prue was delighted to see enough volunteers to make the scheme viable here in Great Plumstead. She quickly noted the names of the women.

'Thank you all, the workers will appreciate you giving your time to help make this work. There's some organising to do before we can start, but I hope we could be up and running in the next month at the latest.'

Prue checked her list before going on. 'Now we're halfway through April our work at the WI allotment is progressing well. We learned so much last year and have used our mistakes and successes to plan for this year. Thank you to all the members who help and if anyone else wants to come along, they're always welcome and for however much time you can spare. And finally, I have a request from the men at our local aerodrome.' Prue glanced at Patsy, who gave her an encouraging smile. 'For some assistance to darn the holes in their socks! They're not very good at it themselves and Group Captain Barlow has requested our help.'

A ripple of amusement spread through the hall, and Prue waited, smiling broadly.

'Of course we can help,' Hettie called out from her seat in the front row. 'We can work on them at The Mother's Day Club.'

'I can darn some at home in the evenings.' Nancy put her hand up and was quickly followed by other women, many of whom were also members of The Mother's Day Club.

'Thank you everyone,' Prue said. 'That's all our business attended to so let's clear the chairs to the side to make room for some games.'

While the women were moving chairs and stacking them at the side of the hall, Patsy came up to Prue, a concerned look on her face.

'Are you sure about darning the socks for the men? Only it sounds like you've all got enough on your plates, what with the allotment and new Rural Pie Scheme plus all the other things you do. Perhaps the men should just learn to do it properly themselves.'

Prue put a hand on the young woman's arm. 'It's fine. We can do it and we want to help. Look at it this way, it's better for the men to do their jobs, repairing the planes, flying them or whatever their job is on the aerodrome, all things that we haven't been trained to do, but we *can* darn their socks. We have the skills to do it properly and they don't. It's just getting a job done in the best, most efficient way.'

'But you have such a lot to do already.'

'Yes, and there'll be more coming along. There always is. But we'll have fun while we work on the socks, being together at The Mother's Day Club, chatting and laughing,' Prue reassured her. 'Now, are you any good at musical chairs? There are some demon players here.'

Patsy looked surprised. 'But that's a children's party game.'

'And one of our favourites for our social part of the meeting,' Prue said. 'We always end with some fun games and singing. It's not all serious stuff about making do and mending. We make sure to mix the business with the light-hearted. We all need some of that in our lives, don't you think?'

Patsy laughed. 'We do. Just wait till the other girls in my Nissen hut hear about tonight's meeting. You might get a whole load more of us turn up next month.'

'And you would all be most welcome,' Prue said. 'Now come on, it's time to play musical chairs!'

CHAPTER 21

'Look at the state of this one!' Gloria held up a sock, poking her finger with its nail painted scarlet through the large gaping hole in the toe. 'It's more 'ole than sock!'

'This one's not much better,' Hettie said, picking a sock off the pile on the table. 'Haven't they ever heard of the saying *a stitch in time saves nine*? A quick mend when a hole first appears and it's a far simpler and smaller job.' She shook her head. 'They've just carried on wearing them, making the holes bigger and bigger.'

Hettie was on duty at The Mother's Day Club this morning and today's task was darning socks for the men from the local aerodrome. Prue had brought in a box of holey socks that had been delivered to her the day before. She'd tipped them out onto a table around which members willing to help with the darning were seated.

'Are you regretting volunteering to darn them now?' Prue asked, taking a sock for herself.

'Of course not, but if you ask me again at the end of the morning, I might not be of the same opinion!' Hettie let out a chuckle. 'If we're going to do this on a regular basis, then we need to get the message across to the men that they must send us their socks to be darned *before* they become this bad.'

'I'll put a note in with the mended socks when they're ready to be collected,' Prue said. 'And I will ask Patsy to spread the word amongst the men as well.'

They settled down to work, deftly mending the gaping holes, sewing in new threads of wool and weaving other threads in and out to form a patch.

'How are the plans going for the Rural Pie Scheme, Prue?' Hettie asked.

'Our baker here in Great Plumstead will take on the extra baking to make the pies,' Prue said. 'So that's sorted. And there's a good list of volunteers. Gloria, I was wondering if you would oversee manning the stall here in the village to start with?'

'Yes, of course,' Gloria agreed.

'Thank you. There will be a couple of you running the stall. I'm working out a rota of those willing to go out to the farms and others who want to stay in the village. If this scheme works well, it will be operating all year round and in all weathers. Some might not be so keen on bicycling out miles to farms in the pouring rain.' Prue pulled a face. 'But it has to be done.'

'At least you're starting it in the spring when the weather's kinder,' Hettie said as she threaded a new length of wool through her darning needle.

'How are you getting on with your role as Land Army Local Representative?' Gloria asked Hettie.

'I'm enjoying it. I went to a farm last week to inspect the accommodation for a possible new Land Girl and the farmer was going to have her sleeping in a barn! I soon put him right on that score,' Hettie said. 'There's a nice room in the farmhouse she'll be having now.'

'The Land Girls would be very welcome at our WI meetings. Do invite them,' Prue said. 'Flo always seems to enjoy herself when she comes along.'

'I'll tell them about it,' Hettie said, thinking it was a good idea and would help Land Girls get to know the community better. It would be especially helpful for those Land Girls who were billeted on their own at a farm.

'Do you remember the days before the war when we just 'ad our homes and families to look after?' Gloria mused. 'They kept me busy enough!'

'The war has brought us a lot more things to do, that's for sure,' Prue agreed. 'But I enjoy doing different things. I've learned so much and met lots of interesting people.'

'You mean people like me?' Gloria let out a throaty cackle. 'I still remember the look on some locals' faces when they first saw me walking down the road in one of my bright dresses...' She smoothed down the skirt of today's fuchsia-pink dress before adding, 'and with my peroxided pompadour 'airstyle and 'igh 'eels. I don't think they'd ever seen anyone like me before!'

'I'm sure they hadn't,' Hettie said with a smile. 'But you've shown them what a lovely person you are and you don't half cheer the place up.'

'Thanks Hettie. I do feel right at 'ome 'ere now. I didn't think that would ever 'appen when I first arrived, but I do.' Gloria blinked as tears made the colour of her brown eyes even brighter. 'Hark at us getting all sentimental while we're darning socks!'

'You and all our evacuees have done well settling in here,' Prue said, giving Gloria's shoulder a squeeze. 'It's difficult being uprooted from your home and sent to live somewhere so different. Remember, we were supposed to have been sent child evacuees but a lucky mistake brought us expectant mothers instead and you've all made a big impact on the village. I'm grateful to whoever put you on the train to Great Plumstead that day, rather than to wherever you should have gone.'

'So am I,' Gloria agreed. 'Now how does that look?' She held up the sock she'd just finished darning. The hole that she'd been able to poke her finger through had been neatly darned and the sock was whole once more.

'Much better,' Hettie said. 'Whoever's sock that is will have much warmer toes now. So that's one sock down – only that lot left to go!' She pointed to the pile in the middle of the table. 'Take your pick.'

CHAPTER 22

The loud ringing broke into Thea's sleep. For a few seconds she wasn't sure if it was in her dream or real. Then with a lurch of her heart, she realised it was the telephone ringing insistently downstairs in the hall. Who could be calling in the middle of the night? Something must be wrong.

Thea threw back her covers, reached for her dressing gown which was draped over the foot of the bedstead and pulled it on. She used the torch she kept in the pocket to check the time on the alarm clock on the bedside stand. It was just after one o'clock.

Hurrying out onto the landing, she almost collided with Hettie. The older woman, like Thea, was wearing her dressing gown and she carried a lit candle, her face shadowed and pinched with worry in the pale flickering candlelight.

'I was on my way to answer it. You go, you're quicker than me,' Hettie said.

Thea ran down the stairs, hoping that the ringing wouldn't stop before she got there.

She snatched up the black Bakelite receiver. 'Hello?'

'Is that Thea Thornton?' a woman's voice asked.

'Yes.'

'Good. I'm telephoning from WVS headquarters in Norwich. I'm sorry to wake you but there's been a massive air raid on Norwich and we're calling in as many canteens from outlying towns as we can. We need to provide food and drink for the fire service battling the fires and rescue parties. Can you bring Wykeham's canteen into the city? It's being prepared by WVS volunteers in Wykeham as I speak and will be ready to go as soon as you can get there.'

Thea didn't hesitate. 'Of course. My sister Prue usually crews it with me.'

'Then bring her too, if she's willing,' the woman said. 'Messengers will be looking out for incoming canteens and will direct you where you need to go. Thank you and good luck.'

Before Thea could say anymore the call was disconnected.

'What's happened?' Hettie had come down the stairs and was hovering in the hallway.

Thea replaced the receiver. 'There's been a huge air raid on Norwich. They're calling in WVS canteens to help.' She gasped, putting a hand to her mouth. 'Oh no, Lizzie! I hope she's safe.'

Hettie patted Thea's arm. 'I'll try to find out about her as soon as I can. Go and get dressed. Is Prue going with you?'

'I don't know yet. I need to telephone her.' Thea's mind was racing with all the things they needed to do.

'I'll see to that while you get ready. Go and get yourself dressed,' Hettie instructed, picking up the telephone and on the prompt from the operator giving Prue's number in the village.

Hurrying upstairs, Thea met Flo and Evie on the landing; both must have also been woken by the telephone. She was glad Marianne and the children hadn't been disturbed as well.

'What's happened?' Flo's face was full of concern.

'Norwich has been bombed and I've been asked to take the WVS canteen there,' Thea quickly told her.

Flo hurried over to the window at the end of the landing, pushed the curtain and the blackout aside and let out a gasp.

'Look!' She pointed out of the window. 'The sky over Norwich is orange.'

Thea and Evie peered out over Flo's shoulder. The sight of the eerie glow in the sky in the direction of Norwich some ten miles away made Thea's heart pound.

'It was like that in the London Blitz,' Evie said solemnly. 'They must have been badly hit.'

Blinking back the tears stinging behind her eyes, Thea hurried to her bedroom to dress in her WVS uniform. The thought of the beautiful city of Norwich being targeted by the Luftwaffe and now on fire was horrifying. It had been attacked before but never on this scale. She vowed to do what she could to help. Serving cups of tea, a fish paste roll or meat pie might not seem much, but if it helped keep firemen going to fight the fires, or rescue workers to dig out casualties, then she was glad to do her bit.

Arriving in the kitchen a short while later, she found Hettie had a cup of tea waiting for her and a thick round of bread and jam. Evie and Flo were making some sandwiches. 'Get this down you before you go. Prue's coming to collect you in her car and drive on to Wykeham to pick up the canteen.'

'Thank you,' Thea said gratefully, before taking a sip of tea and tucking into the bread and jam. She wasn't hungry but she didn't know when she might next get a chance to have something, so it was wise to eat while she could.

'We thought you should take some sandwiches with you.' Hettie indicated Flo and Evie.

'Good idea. Thank you.'

~

By the time Prue arrived, Thea was ready to leave. Dressed in her WVS green coat and hat, she'd been waiting by the front door watching for her sister's car to pull in through the gate.

'Mind how you go and take care,' Hettie said, grabbing hold of Thea's arm as she opened the door. 'Don't worry about anything here. I'll see everything gets done with the help of the others. You just look after yourself and Prue.' The older woman's voice wavered.

'Thank you, Hettie.' Thea gave her friend a swift hug. 'We'll be careful. I promise.'

Striding out into the night with the basket of food and drink, Thea hurried to Prue's car and got in, pleased to see an almost full moon lighting her way.

'Are you ready for this?' Prue asked, glancing at Thea as she put the car into gear and headed for the gateway.

'As ready as I'll ever be. It was a shock and not the best way to be woken up.'

'No, it wasn't. And I had Victor moaning about it until I told him what was going on and why. You should have seen the look on his face when I said there'd been a big raid on Norwich – the colour literally drained away.'

'He must be worried about his mistress.'

Prue waved her hand as if swatting away the idea. 'It's Lizzie I'm worried for, but there's nothing we can do about that now. Our job is to get the canteen to Norwich as fast as we can. I'm grateful the WVS has a petrol allowance for its work – otherwise we'd be having to bicycle to Wykeham, which would take even longer!'

~

After picking up the canteen that was ready for them at Wykeham, they made good speed but even so the drive to Norwich seemed to take forever. Thea was glad when they finally reached the outskirts of the city at Hellesdon. At least the moonlight had made driving easier and lit up the road ahead. They hadn't had to crawl along at a slow snail's pace as would have been the case if they'd only been relying on the limited light given out by the cowled headlights.

'The nearer we get, the worse it looks.' Prue stared out of the windscreen at the sky above the city, which had an otherworldly orange glow to it. 'I dread to think what it's like in the centre. Do you think anything's left standing?'

Thea bit her bottom lip. 'I don't know. I hope so. I can't help thinking about Lizzie, it...' Her voice cracked.

Prue reached across the cab and put her hand on Thea's arm. 'I know. Try not to think the worst. She's sensible and will have gone to a shelter when the air-raid siren sounded.'

'But shelters can take a direct hit.' Thea blinked away tears.

'I know it's worrying, but we need to focus on the job in hand,' Prue said in a firm voice.

'You're right.' Thea threw her sister a small smile, slowing the canteen as they approached a junction. 'It's going to be a busy night.'

As they got nearer to the centre of Norwich, the fires glowed brighter, lighting up the streets as bright as day, but with an eerie orange tint. They had no problem spotting a waiting messenger standing in the middle of the road who signalled for them to stop.

Bringing the canteen to a halt, Thea wound down the window in the driver's door. 'We're WVS from Wykeham,' she informed the young man.

'Glad you've come to help.' He managed a half-smile, his teeth white in his soot-smudged face. 'Can you head towards City Station and set up somewhere safe around there? The station's an inferno and they're fighting to control it. There'll be ARP volunteers in the area to help you. Mind how you go, there's a lot of debris on the roads in some places.'

'Will do, thanks.' Thea wound up the window, waving as the messenger gave a salute and stepped back to the side of the road, motioning them onwards with a swing of his arm.

'City Station on fire!' Prue exclaimed. 'It's hard to believe. How many times over the years have we arrived there on the train?' She let out a sigh. 'Norwich is going to look a lot different after this raid and that's just one place we know of that's been hit tonight.'

Following the messenger's instructions Thea drove them towards the City Station area, taking care to go slowly on the increasingly rubble-strewn roads. She'd never been so grateful for her experience driving an ambulance in France during the Great War. Back then, the roads had often been potholed and uneven and she'd had injured men in the back whose pain would be multiplied by jolts and bumps.

Keeping her eyes peeled on the road, the light from fires and the moon helping, Thea was relieved when they finally arrived at their destination. An ARP man spotted them and waved them to a parking place a safe distance from the station.

As soon as she jumped out of the cab, Thea was hit by the smell of burning and the roar of flames from the stricken station. Black silhouettes of firemen battled to control the blaze, aiming their hoses with jets of water pumped from the nearby River Wensum.

On the other side of the road, buildings had been destroyed, crumpled into piles of rubble with beams of wood sticking out like matchsticks.

'You're a welcome sight,' the ARP man said. 'A cup of tea and bite to eat will seem like the food of the gods after dealing with this lot.'

'We'll get up and running as quick as we can,' Thea assured him, heading around to the back of the canteen. She was acutely aware of crunching under her shoes and looked down to see tiny, glittering pieces of glass blown out of windows by the force of the blasts. The might of war had hit Norwich and its people hard tonight.

The next few hours passed in a blur for Thea. She was thankful for her and Prue's experience running the canteen on their trips out to the searchlight batteries or on invasion exercises. All those previous times had honed their methods and now allowed them to work smoothly and seamlessly like a well-oiled machine. They'd hardly stopped since they'd opened the shutter at the front of the canteen, ready to serve. There had been a steady stream of customers desperate for a drink and something to eat before returning to their work. They'd served fire crew, first aiders, rescue workers, ARP and policemen, all of them glad of a break and chance to refuel.

'Thanks for that.' A fireman placed his used mug on the counter, his face blackened with soot. 'My throat was parched.'

'How's it going at the station?' Thea asked.

He gave a sad shake of his head. 'We're doing the best we can but it's a heck of a mess. The fire took hold so quickly and soon became an inferno. There's a lot of wood and fabric to burn in the carriages. But we'll keep at it.' With a nod of thanks, he turned and made his way back to join his fellow firemen still tackling the blaze.

Thea and Prue had somehow kept going through the long hours of the night, eating the food they'd brought with them on the go as there'd been no chance to take breaks. Their supplies had been restocked by local WVS volunteers who'd delivered more sandwiches, pies and water so they didn't run out.

As the sun rose, it bathed the devastation of bombed-out buildings in pale light, highlighting the grey pall of smoke hanging over the city. It was shocking to see a place they were so familiar with now reduced to rubble, ash and twisted and blackened metalwork.

It was mid-afternoon when two other WVS members from Wykeham arrived to take over running the canteen. Glad to hand over to them, Thea and Prue made their way to a station further out of the city to catch a train back to Wykeham where they'd pick up Prue's car and finally head for home.

'I'm exhausted.' Thea slumped against the springy seat as the train began to move. 'I didn't feel it while we kept going but now...' She held up both her hands. 'It's hit me. I don't think we stopped in all that time in the canteen. How many cups of tea do you reckon we served?'

'Plenty, and each one of them was gratefully received. What a night!' Prue let out a heavy sigh. 'I'm glad we went to help. What we did was small in comparison with the firemen or the rescue workers, but we played a part.'

Thea nodded. 'We did. Though I wish it hadn't been necessary. We need to find out about Lizzie. I hope she's all right. It's shocking to see what's happened to Norwich and its people.'

CHAPTER 23

Hettie listened to the sound of ringing, willing the phone to be picked up. She had lost count of the number of times she'd tried calling the Land Army Office in Castle Street, Norwich where Lizzie worked. With Lizzie not having a telephone in her home, this was the only place Hettie could reach her. Five more rings, she thought, but as she counted off the last one, there was still no answer, so regretfully she replaced the receiver and made her way into the kitchen.

Since the telephone call in the middle of the night, followed by Thea rushing off with Prue to take the WVS canteen into Norwich, Hettie hadn't slept. She'd gone back to bed after Thea had left, but her mind wouldn't be still, worrying and thinking about what she'd need to organise for the day ahead. Getting the children up and off to school, making sure Flo and Nancy knew what they were doing and that all the animals were tended to, Primrose milked and so on. It had all been fine but now at half past two in the afternoon, Hettie's lack of sleep was catching up with her and the thought of a quick nap was tempting.

Settling herself down in the chair by the range, Hettie had almost dropped off when the telephone began to ring in the hall. Coming to with a start, she hurried to answer it.

'Hello, Rookery House,' she said.

'Hettie!' Lizzie's voice came down the line, bringing a rush of tears to Hettie's eyes. 'Have you heard about the bombing last night here in Norwich?'

'Lizzie, thank goodness.' Hettie let out a long sigh, her shoulders dropping in relief. 'I've been trying to reach you at the Land Army office. And yes, we know, we saw the sky aglow over the city. Thea and Prue are there with the WVS canteen.'

'I've only just got into the office. The city's been badly hit and it took me a while to get in. You should see the place, so much destroyed.' Lizzie's voice caught and she halted for a moment. 'It was scary, Hettie, far worse than anything we've had before.'

'What happened?'

'The siren went off about twenty-five past eleven last night. It woke me up. I saw flares coming down as I hurried to next door's shelter. They lit up the sky so brightly it was like daylight. The bombers would have had no trouble finding the city after that. The drone of the planes was horrible, made my blood run cold and the scream and thump of bombs. The anti-aircraft guns were booming as well. What a cacophony!' She halted for a moment before adding, 'It was over by a quarter to one this morning, but it seemed to last for much longer.'

'You're not hurt, are you?' Hettie asked.

'No, not at all. Only a bit shaky after missing out on sleep and being scared. I am fine, all in one piece and my house wasn't damaged at all. Other houses not so far away weren't as lucky. Anyway, I thought I must telephone, as I knew you'd be worried. Please tell everyone I'm unhurt. I need to check on other staff who haven't come in yet.'

'I will and thank you for telephoning. Hearing you're all right is a huge weight off my mind.'

After they ended the call, Hettie returned to the kitchen and settled back in the chair, this time with a lighter heart. Soon she drifted away and was woken only by the sound of Marianne arriving home with the children from school sometime later that afternoon.

CHAPTER 24

It was the last day of April and, only a couple of days after the huge raid on Norwich, Prue and Thea were back in the city with the WVS canteen. The Luftwaffe had returned to bomb again late last night and once more the sisters had been called out in the early hours of the morning.

Now after a long shift of over twelve hours serving countless cups of tea, rounds of sandwiches and pies to fire crews and other civil defence workers, Prue was glad to see a pair of familiar faces. Two other WVS volunteers from Wykeham had arrived to take over running the canteen and they were relieved of their duty.

'I need to check something before we head home,' Prue told her sister as they gathered their things from the cab of the canteen after handing over to the new crew. 'I'm tired, but I've got a strange niggling feeling and I know if I don't follow it up, I'll regret it.'

'What's the matter?' Thea looked concerned.

'We're close to where Victor's mistress lives. Remember

how we followed him there from City Station with Lizzie, so I could see what he was getting up to and with who?'

Thea nodded. 'You think it might have been bombed?'

Prue looked at the surrounding devastation. This area of the city near St Benedict's Gate, where they'd been instructed to set up the canteen, had been badly hit with many buildings reduced to rubble. The damage went out along the Dereham Road and into the city centre, so a fireman had told them whilst having a cup of tea.

'I don't know, but I've got this weird feeling and it won't go away.' Prue put a hand over her chest. 'Not that I should be worried about Victor's mistress…'

'We can go and look – it's not that far from here, but it won't be as straightforward a walk as the last time we went,' Thea warned her. 'We'll have to work our way around rubble.'

'Thank you.' Prue was relieved that she wouldn't have to do this alone. She didn't know what had got into her, only that an odd feeling of *something* had been growing since they'd arrived in Norwich, when the sky had been lit by the orange glow from the fires raging out of control over the city. The air had smelt of burning and billows of smoke had risen up, smudging the light of the full moon.

It took them a while to reach the street where Victor's mistress lived. Prue was glad they were in their WVS uniforms as their progress went unchallenged by other civil defence workers, no doubt thinking they were on official WVS business. Their way had been frequently blocked where buildings had crumpled, spilling rubble and dust out over the road. The sound of glass crunching under her feet made Prue wince and seeing houses blown apart was shocking. One had half a bedroom open to the air, a curtain flapping in the breeze and a smashed child's cot hanging over the edge where the outside wall had once been. It was horrifying how people's homes and lives had been altered in a moment by a falling bomb. Prue hoped that whoever lived in that house had gone to a shelter and wasn't buried somewhere under the remains of their home.

As they approached the end of the street, Prue could see a rescue party working up ahead, painstakingly digging in the rubble. They had just brought someone out of the ruins and were laying them down on a stretcher.

'It was around there, wasn't it?' Thea pointed to the rescue party. 'Do you know what number?'

'Six, I think.' Prue looked at the few remaining numbered front doors and calculated where six should be. Only it wasn't there anymore, and neither were numbers four or eight. The houses had crumbled into rubble, remains of walls jutting out and wooden beams protruding at odd angles.

'Can you come and help over here for a few minutes?' an ARP warden called to them as he and another man carried the figure on the stretcher away from the house to a safer, clearer area and laid it on the ground.

Prue and Thea hurried over.

'This woman's just been dug out,' the warden said. 'Didn't go to the shelter like she ought to have done.' He frowned, pursing his lips with his demeanour full of disapproval under his steel helmet. 'Keep her talking till the ambulance arrives. We need to keep her conscious if we can.'

'Of course.' Prue glanced at Thea, who nodded in agreement.

Prue looked down at the woman and drew in a sharp breath. Despite the layer of gritty brick and plaster dust covering her face, hair and clothes, there was no doubt that this was Victor's mistress. Prue had seen her with Victor the day they'd followed him.

Thea must have sensed her sister's reaction as she grabbed

hold of Prue's arm, a questioning look on her face as their eyes met. Prue gave a discreet motion of her head downwards and watched as Thea stared in disbelief at the woman lying prone on the stretcher.

'Oh Prue...' Thea whispered, her hand flying up to cover her mouth.

Prue gave a single decisive nod, then took a deep breath and lifted her chin. The woman was hurt and, even though she was committing adultery with Prue's husband, Prue could not abandon her.

'Hello.' Prue knelt beside the stretcher, forcing a smile. 'What's your name?'

'Miriam. Miriam Roper.' The woman's voice was hoarse.

'It won't be long before the ambulance comes to take you to hospital, then they'll soon get you fixed up,' Prue said kindly.

'I thought we'd be safe under the kitchen table...' Tears rolled down Miriam's cheek, making a trail in the dust. 'I didn't want to go to the shelter so we stayed put.'

'We? Was there someone else in there with you?' Thea asked, crouching down on the other side of the stretcher.

Miriam nodded. 'Yes, my Vic. He came to stay with me because I was so scared after the big raid the other night. Where is he?'

Prue glanced at Thea, her own alarm mirrored on her sister's face.

They didn't have a chance to question Miriam further as two ambulance crew arrived and quickly carried the injured woman off to the waiting ambulance, which was parked as close as they could get it.

'Did you know Victor had come here?' Thea asked.

'No. I've hardly seen him since early Tuesday morning

118

when Hettie telephoned to say we'd been called out. I went to bed soon after we got back and he'd already left for work when I got up yesterday,' Prue said. 'He rang about five last night to tell me he had a meeting to go to and wouldn't be home till late. I presumed he'd come back after I'd gone to sleep. No wonder he didn't appear when the phone rang early this morning. I thought he must have slept through it...' She let out a heavy sigh. 'But he wasn't even at home – he was here in Norwich!'

'He must still be in there. Are they even looking for him? The ARP wardens have a list of who lives in each house in a street and if Victor's name's not on it, they won't expect him to be there.'

'If they don't know, then they'll leave him there!' Prue dashed over to the warden. He was talking to the rescue workers who'd halted their digging.

'The woman... Miriam, told us there was another person in there with her – he's called Vic.' Saying the shortened version of Victor's name felt alien on Prue's tongue.

The warden took a notebook out of the top pocket of his overalls and consulted it. 'No, just says a Miss M. Roper lives at number six. You sure she said there was somebody else in there with her?'

'Yes. Her friend came to see her because she was scared. He must still be in there.' Prue looked imploringly at the rescue workers who'd been listening to their conversation.

'Come on lads, there's someone else needs rescuing,' the leader said, giving instructions before they began a careful dig through the ruins.

Prue waited, her arms folded around her body. Never in a million years would she have expected to find herself in this situation. But here she was, waiting for her husband to be dug out of his mistress's house.

'Are you all right?' Thea asked gently, coming to stand beside her.

Prue gave a nod. 'Do you think he's alive?'

'I don't know. Miriam is – she's hurt, but she survived. There's…' Thea didn't finish what she was about to say because a shout went up from the rescue workers. They'd discovered something.

Prue watched, stock-still, her heart thudding hard inside her chest, as they brought a man out of the ruins of Miriam's house and laid him on a stretcher. To her surprise, she found herself running towards them, aware that her sister was close behind.

'Who is it? Can I see?'

The men laid the stretcher down and Prue gazed at the figure lying on it. His icy blue eyes stared sightlessly up at the sky. It was Victor and he was dead.

Prue put a hand to her mouth, stifling a gasp.

'Do you know him?' one of the rescue workers asked.

She nodded.

'His name is Victor Wilson,' Thea informed them as she slipped her arm through Prue's. 'He lives in Great Plumstead. I can give you his address.'

Aware of her sister telling the ARP warden details in the background, Prue watched in fascination as the other man covered Victor with a blanket. It was as if she were seeing this from afar, as if it were happening to another person. The thought that it was *her* husband lying there dead, killed while with his mistress, and that she was here to see him carried out of the place he'd been entombed by a bomb was unbelievable.

'What will happen to him?' Prue managed to ask, blankly.

'He'll be taken to the mortuary and his next of kin will be informed,' the ARP man told them as he filled in a label with Victor's name and address on. Then he moved the blanket to the side and threaded the string of the label through a buttonhole in Victor's dust-covered jacket.

Prue nodded. She could say that *she* was his next of kin but the words wouldn't come out. They might ask what he was doing here. Why he'd been in a house with another woman who'd been asking for him after she'd been brought out. It was better to say nothing. Prue had seen enough.

'Can we go now?' she asked Thea.

'Come on.' Thea put her arm around Prue's shoulders and led her away. 'I'm taking you home with me to Rookery House.'

CHAPTER 25

As she drove Prue's car home from Wykeham, Thea kept glancing at her sister who sat silently in the passenger seat, staring straight ahead through the windscreen. Since they'd witnessed Victor's body being brought out of the ruins of his mistress's house, and identified him, Prue had said very little. Throughout the journey back from Norwich, first to Wykeham on the train and now the last leg in the car, Prue hadn't said a word, her face in a set, neutral expression, looking as if it were made from the palest alabaster.

Her sister was in shock, Thea thought, returning her attention to the road. And it wasn't surprising after discovering her husband like that, killed while with his mistress. Prue and Victor hadn't been close, but even so, to see it happen like that was still dreadful. Prue was going to need looking after and that was why Thea was taking her to Rookery House, rather than straight to Prue's own home in the village.

Thea had telephoned from the station on the outskirts of Norwich to tell Hettie what had happened and asked her to light the copper so there was plenty of hot water for Prue to have a bath. Some good home comforts – a bath, delicious, comforting food and then to be tucked up in bed was what was needed this evening. A first step in helping Prue recover from the shock.

Thea stifled a yawn, her exhaustion creeping up on her the nearer she got to home. She'd been tired after the long shift working at the canteen, but the discovery of Victor's death and need to take care of her sister had galvanised her into digging deep to find a reserve of energy. Now that was fast running out.

Finally turning into the gateway of Rookery House, she cut the engine with a sigh of relief.

'Prue.' Thea touched her sister's arm and she started as if woken from a trance. 'We're home.'

Prue gave a nod, her eyes looking hollow in her face.

Thea got out of the car and went round to the passenger's side to help her sister out. Then with her arm around Prue's waist, she led her to the back door where they were met by a bustling Hettie.

'Flo's got the bath running for you – started it as soon as we saw you pull in through the gateway.' Hettie took hold of Prue's hands. 'I'm sorry to hear what's happened.'

Prue nodded and took off her coat, clearly not wanting to say anything.

Thea caught Hettie's eye, a look of understanding passing between them.

'I'll take over from here, Thea. You look exhausted too. I've changed the sheets on your bed and made up the camp bed beside it for you to sleep on, just as you asked,' Hettie said. 'The children are asleep. We put them to bed a little earlier than usual. Thought it best, so it was quiet when you got back.'

'Thank you.' Thea's eyes filled with tears as she felt the

warmth of Hettie's care and the security of Rookery House wrap around her. She hoped being here would help Prue too.

Flo appeared in the doorway that led to the scullery and the bathroom. 'The bath's nearly ready.'

'Good, thank you, Flo.' Hettie hooked her arm through Prue's and steered her away towards the bathroom.

'Hettie told me what happened,' Flo said to Thea, her voice sympathetic. 'If there's anything I can do...'

'It was a terrible shock.' Thea pulled a chair out from the table and slumped down onto it, putting her elbows on the tabletop and resting her head in her hands.

'What was Prue's husband doing in Norwich?' Flo asked.

Thea remained with her head in her hands for a few moments, thinking that this innocent question was one many people would ask when they heard what had happened. They had no idea that Victor had a woman there and would be outraged if they knew the truth. Victor's image of local businessman and member of many committees and the Home Guard would not sit well alongside having a secret mistress. For Prue's sake, it was best that the real reason for Victor's presence in Norwich during the raid didn't become widely known. Only she, Lizzie, Prue and Hettie knew about Miriam. Thea had let Hettie in on the secret when she'd telephoned earlier, so she would understand the significance of today's events.

'He must have been to a meeting,' Thea said, raising her head, 'and was unlucky to have been caught there when the Luftwaffe attacked.'

'Poor Alice. She won't know yet,' Flo said, thinking of her friend.

'I'll talk to Prue about sending telegrams to Alice and her brothers tomorrow. Then there'll be a funeral to arrange...' Thea slowly shook her head. 'But all that can wait. Rest is what Prue needs now and so do I. It feels an age since I left here in the early hours of this morning.'

'Do you want some soup? Hettie's made some and it's delicious as always. And there's fresh bread and butter to go with it.' Flo pointed at the saucepan keeping warm on top of the range.

A bowl of Hettie's soup with bread and butter sounded just what Thea needed right now. 'Yes please, that sounds good.' She went to stand up to organise some for herself and Prue.

'You stay there. I'll see to it.' Flo put her hand on Thea's shoulder. 'It won't take me a minute.'

'Thank you.'

Thea was eating her soup when Hettie came through from the bathroom a few minutes later, carrying Prue's clothes in her arms. 'Prue's in the bath having a soak,' Hettie said. 'I've left her one of your clean nightgowns and a dressing gown to put on if that's all right?'

'Of course.' Thea nodded. 'Thank you, Hettie. I hope Prue will have something to eat when she's finished. It's ages since she last ate and the sandwiches we took with us had to be eaten in snatched five minute breaks. It was so busy at the canteen again. Then after... well, she didn't want anything on the way home.'

'Prue's had a horrible shock. Things like that are enough to rob anyone of their appetite. Probably wisest not to force her. She'll eat when she's hungry,' Hettie said wisely. 'Sleep is the best thing for Prue at the moment.'

Lying in her camp bed, Thea listened to the steady sound of Prue's breathing, thankful that her sister had fallen asleep within moments of getting into bed, both her mind and body exhausted by the day's events. Thea, however, was having difficulty sleeping despite the heaviness of exhaustion weighing her body down, because her mind would not surrender to sleep. It kept going over and over their shocking discovery. Replaying seeing Prue's face when she'd recognised Victor's mistress, the news that Victor was in the bombed house and then finally, the removal of Victor's body from the rubble and identifying him. It had been like something out of a film. It hadn't felt real, and yet it was. What had happened would send Prue's life on a different course. Thea didn't want to consider that yet. Right now, the most important thing was to support her sister and be there for her.

At least the good news from Hettie that Lizzie was safe and well was a relief and one less thing to worry about. Thea turned onto her side and plumped up her pillow before resting her head on it again. Think of something else, she told herself and pictured walking around the grounds of Rookery House, looking at the garden, heading over towards Primrose's field to watch the gentle cow grazing on the fresh green spring grass. Slowly, Thea felt her body relax and, at last, sleep claimed her.

CHAPTER 26

As Prue slowly drifted into wakefulness, it took a few moments for her to register the sound of another person in the room. The rhythmic breathing of someone sleeping came from her right. Prue's heart raced. Who was it? Not Victor. It had been a long time since they'd shared a bedroom.

She rolled onto her side and peered over the edge of the bed. In the dim light, she could just make out Thea lying fast asleep beside her on a camp bed. Prue realised she wasn't at home. This wasn't her bedroom. Then yesterday's events came rushing back, thumping her squarely in the chest. Victor was dead! Killed while at his mistress's home in Norwich.

Prue rolled onto her back and lay still, staring up at the ceiling as images played in her head like a film reel. The sight of Victor's mistress – Miriam Roper – lying on a stretcher talking about *my Vic*. Then Victor being pulled from the ruins of Miriam's house, killed by an enemy bomb when he should have been safely at home in Great Plumstead.

She couldn't recall anything of the journey back here to Rookery House. Prue only had vague memories of the kindness of Hettie and Thea. The soothing heat of the bathwater. Being tucked up in a bed warmed by hot water bottles. But now the shock of yesterday's discovery hit her like a steam train going at full pelt. Why had she wanted to see if Victor's mistress's house had been damaged? Had she known deep down her husband might be there?

Prue remembered how something had niggled at her while she'd been serving in the canteen, how it had compelled her to go and look. If she hadn't followed that gut feeling, then how would she have found out about what had happened to Victor? Presumably, the village constable would have brought the news to her. Was it better that she had been there to see it for herself? she wondered.

From the short time she'd spent with Miriam, it was clear that she loved Victor. Maybe the feeling was mutual. If he'd gone there to stay with Miriam because she was scared, it showed he cared for her. Prue could never imagine him doing the same for her. Victor must have shown another side of himself to Miriam, one he'd never revealed to Prue in all the years they were together. She'd thought him incapable of such emotions. Perhaps there was something about Miriam that was different, brought out Victor's loving side. It was curious and strangely fascinating. Prue wanted to know more.

Thea stirred in her bed and said in a sleepy voice, 'Are you awake?'

'Yes,' Prue answered.

'How are you?'

How was she? Prue considered the question, imagining herself prodding at her heart to get some reaction out of it because it felt numb. There was no sadness, no anger – it was just there as usual doing its job.

'I'm fine.' Prue pulled herself up into a seated position. 'I must get home. Alice, Jack and Edwin need to be told what's happened. Best to send them telegrams.'

'If you tell me what you want to say, I can do that for you,' Thea said.

'No, I'd rather do it myself, but thank you.' Prue swung her legs out of the bed. 'I'll get up now and go. Thank you for everything, Thea. For yesterday and bringing me to stay here. But now I really must leave. I have things to see to.'

'Prue, wait!' Thea struggled out of the low camp bed and grabbed hold of Prue's arm. 'You're in shock.'

'Perhaps, but there are still things to organise. It's better than sitting around staring at the wall, don't you think?' Seeing the surprised look on her sister's face Prue added, 'You know me, I like to be busy.'

Back at her own home, Prue was forcing down some toast and blackberry jam, even though she didn't feel hungry, when Nancy came into the kitchen.

'Prue, you're back!' Nancy hurried across the room and wrapped her in a warm embrace, before stepping back and still holding onto Prue's upper arms asking ''ow are you? I was sorry to 'ear what 'appened. Thea rang last night to let me know you'd be staying at Rookery 'ouse with her.'

'Did she?' Prue knew Thea would have told her what she was doing but had no recollection of it. 'I'm fine, thank you.'

'I didn't expect you back so soon. Thea said she was going to look after you for a while,' Nancy said.

'I'm fine, honestly, and I wanted to come home. In fact, I should be on duty at The Mother's Day Club this morning, but...'

'No need to worry about that,' Nancy interrupted. 'I'll give

Gloria a ring – see if she'll take over for you there. I'd do it myself if I wasn't working at Rookery House. I'm sure Gloria will be glad to 'elp. You'll need some time to take in what's 'appened.'

Prue nodded. 'Thank you, I appreciate that. I have things to organise, telegrams to send to inform the children and...' Her voice tailed off as she didn't want to tell Nancy the crazy idea that had been growing inside ever since she'd woken up and felt like an itch that needing scratching. The more she thought about it, the more she wanted to do it. Prue knew if she confided in anyone about it, they were bound to try to dissuade her. But she needed to know more. To dig deeper, to understand why. It was for her own sanity and then she could put it all to rest and move on.

'Fair enough,' her friend said. 'But if there's anything else I can 'elp you with just say, won't yer?'

'I will, thank you.' Prue gave her friend an appreciative smile, glad more than ever to have Nancy and her daughters living with her.

Prue stood outside the front of the Norfolk and Norwich Hospital staring up at the red brick façade, hoping that somewhere inside she might find answers to her questions.

After sending telegrams from the village post office, she'd come into the city again on her own, catching the train from Great Plumstead. Even though she'd been here just yesterday and seen the destruction brought about by the Norwich Blitz, it had still shocked her to see so many familiar buildings in ruins. The department stores on Rampant Horse Street and St Stephens had been destroyed. Even the chocolate factory had been hit. The city was still reeling from the air raids and it would take a long time to clear up the damage and recover. The place would never be the same again. Rather like her, Prue thought. The attack on Norwich had changed her life too.

Taking several slow, steadying breaths, Prue lifted her chin, went in through the front doors and headed for the reception desk.

'Good morning,' Prue said to the bespectacled woman who manned the desk. 'I've come to see Miss Miriam Roper. Could you tell me which ward she's on, please?'

The receptionist looked Prue up and down, taking in her clean WVS uniform dress, which she'd changed into before leaving home. Satisfied at what she saw, she said, 'One moment,' and checked the register. 'You'll find Miss Roper on Heigham Ward.'

'Thank you.' Prue gave the woman a smile and headed for the ward, following the signs. Her plan to wear her WVS uniform had worked as it was otherwise unlikely she'd be admitted without it, not being next of kin. A small dart of guilt had prickled Prue when she'd had the idea, as she wasn't here on official WVS business, but then she'd been wearing her uniform when she'd helped keep Miriam awake and it would help the woman recognise her again.

Arriving at Heigham Ward, Prue had a quick word with the staff nurse on duty and was pointed towards Miriam's bed.

Walking down the ward to where Miriam lay, Prue had a flicker of doubt at the sanity of what she was about to do but stamped it down firmly. If she didn't take this opportunity, then she would always wonder.

'Good morning, Miss Roper, Miriam. Do you remember me?' Prue asked as she halted at the end of the woman's bed.

Miriam frowned, then her face cleared. 'You were there

after they pulled me out of my house. You and the other WVS woman talked to me.'

'That's right. Can I sit down?' Prue gestured towards a nearby chair. 'I came to see how you are.'

Miriam nodded.

Prue pulled the chair up beside the bed and sat down. 'How are you?'

'Battered and bruised and...' Miriam's voice wavered. 'Heart-broken.' Fat tears spilled over and ran down her cheeks. 'My Vic... he's dead!' she hiccupped through her sobs.

Prue summoned every ounce of her inner strength to hold herself in, to maintain a calm exterior, to act the part. 'I'm sorry for your loss. You told us he was in the remains of your house so we informed the ARP warden; otherwise they wouldn't have looked for him. The warden thought it was only you living there.'

Miriam sniffed, nodding. 'It would have been only me normally. But I was scared after the big raid the other night and Vic came to be with me, to stay. When the siren went, we decided to shelter under the table in the kitchen. We thought we'd be all right under there but then there was this loud bang, it went black and I could smell the dust in the air. I called to him. "Vic," I kept saying. "Talk to me, Vic," but he never answered.'

'So Vic wasn't your husband?' Prue queried, her hands clasped in her lap, squeezing her fingers together hard.

'Not yet. He was my fiancé,' Miriam said and Prue had to stifle a gasp. 'We were getting married after the war. I didn't want to wait until then, however long it might be, but Vic said we should, that it would be less busy then, safer...' More tears welled in her eyes and slid down her cheeks. 'I wish we hadn't waited.'

Prue couldn't trust herself to speak for a few moments, her

anger at Victor bubbling inside her. It was bad enough him having a mistress but to have proposed to her, let her believe he was free to marry... It was despicable behaviour towards both her and Miriam.

'No one knows what the future holds,' Prue managed at last. 'He couldn't have known what would happen to him.'

'We should have grabbed the chance to be together while we could.' Miriam kneaded the top of the white sheet covering her with her fingers. 'If we'd been married, then I'd have moved out to live at his house in Wykeham and we wouldn't have been in Norwich in the raid. Vic would still be alive now.'

He hadn't even told Miriam the truth about where he lived, Prue thought. 'Did he live alone there?' she asked.

'No, he's got a housekeeper called Prudence. He said she's a real dragon but keeps the house well. Vic felt sorry for her and didn't want to give her notice so he let her stay. He was a kind man like that. Once we were married though, I would have given her notice. I just wanted it to be me looking after him.'

Prue stared at the woman who'd been spun a tangled web of lies and deceit by Victor. 'Did Vic have any family?'

'No, it was just him. He'd never thought of marrying before he met me, so he told me. But I changed all that for him.' She gave a sad smile. 'He was a lonely bachelor, busy with his business and committees. That's how we met. I'm a secretary and took minutes at one of the meetings and it was like he was the only man in the room for me.' Miriam let out a sigh. 'We were meant for each other and now...'

The rattle of the tea trolley at the other end of the ward caught Prue's attention. Reeling from what she'd just heard, she stood up. 'I'll get you some tea.'

Prue hardly listened to the nurse as she poured two cups of tea out for her. She nodded and smiled her thanks, but all the while her mind was sifting through what Miriam had said.

The lies Victor had told to his so-called fiancé had erased so much from his life, his children and Prue, even where he lived. Miriam had clearly trusted him and had no reason to doubt what he'd told her. Victor had lived a double life, lying to both Prue and Miriam. What would he have done if he'd survived to the end of the war? Prue wondered. Would he have kept stringing Miriam along with excuses to avoid marrying her and exposing his lies, or would he have divorced Prue so he could marry his mistress? Prue would never now know.

As she carried the cups of tea back to Miriam's bed, Prue felt a growing sense of pity for Miriam. The woman didn't seem like a husband stealer. She appeared genuine and had been taken in and used by a manipulating, dominating liar. What would telling her the truth do to her? Might it be better to let her continue to believe she was truly loved?

In her heart, Prue didn't feel it was right to tell Miriam the truth after what she had discovered, for the simple reason it would only hurt her further. It was kinder to protect Miriam, leave her with some dignity rather than destroy what she thought she'd had. Victor had done enough damage and Prue would not add to it. She'd found answers to her questions and understood as much as she could now.

'A nice cup of tea for you,' she said, handing a cup to Miriam, then sitting down beside the bed again to drink her own. 'Where are you going to go when you're discharged?'

'My sister's. But that won't be for a few days, so they've told me. I won't be able to go to Vic's funeral.' Her voice cracked.

At least having Miriam turn up at the funeral was something Prue wouldn't have to worry about, she thought with relief. Changing the subject she asked, 'Where does your sister live?'

'In Wroxham. I'll stay with her for a bit. I will start again somehow.' Miriam gave a little lift of her shoulders. 'Vic wouldn't have wanted me to be sad forever. He was such a cheerful man.'

'Was he?' Prue couldn't help an ironic smile forming on her lips. The Victor Miriam knew was a world away from the one Prue had lived with.

'Yes, I'll treasure my memories of him.' Miriam took a sip of her tea, her eyes welling up with tears again.

Prue took a drink of her own tea, thinking her own memories of Victor were not ones to treasure. The best thing she could do now was to put him firmly behind her and forge a new future for herself. Victor could no longer dominate her, make her feel bad or spoil the happiness in their home. Coming here today had revealed the truth and allowed Prue to put things into perspective. It had been necessary and cathartic.

'I hope in time you'll start afresh. I really do.' Prue's eyes met Miriam's and she reached out and patted the woman's hand.

CHAPTER 27

Thea was worried. She hadn't liked the idea of Prue going home on her own this morning but had respected her sister's decision and planned to check on her later. Only now the problem was that Prue was nowhere to be found. Nobody Thea had spoken to knew where she was. Keeping her eyes peeled as she cycled along, Thea had run out of places to look for her in the village.

Earlier this afternoon she'd headed to Prue's house expecting to find her there but no one was at home. The next obvious place to try was the village hall in case Prue had gone to The Mother's Day Club. But there Thea had been told by Gloria that she was standing in for Prue and, like Thea, she'd thought Prue was at home. Next Thea had tried the WI allotment, then gone down by the river where her sister liked to walk and finally asked in all the shops, but Prue hadn't been in any of those places. Where was she?

Perhaps she'd gone to Rookery House and somehow they'd missed each other. Deciding to head home to check, Thea was bicycling towards Great Plumstead station when she spotted a familiar figure emerging from its entrance. It was Prue and she was dressed in her green WVS uniform.

'Prue!' Thea waved at her sister and peddled fast to reach her. 'I've been looking for you.' She braked and dismounted. 'Are you all right? I was worried when I couldn't find you.'

'I've been to Norwich,' Prue said matter of factly.

Thea frowned. 'Why? Did you go back to volunteer at a canteen?'

'No. I went to the hospital to see Miriam Roper.'

Thea couldn't speak for a few seconds. 'I don't understand. Why on earth would you want to do that?'

'Because I had to. I *needed* to know.' Prue put her hand on Thea's elbow. 'We need to talk but not here. Let's head back to Rookery House; its quieter that way and I don't want to be overheard.'

They fell into step, walking alongside each other, with Thea pushing her bicycle. She was bursting with questions about why Prue would visit Victor's mistress. She ought to be the last person her sister wanted to see.

'The thing is, I needed to know why Victor was there with her, what was going on between them? It felt like my only chance,' Prue explained once they'd left the village behind. 'I went in my role as one of the WVS women who'd helped Miriam yesterday and was there checking on how she was doing. She didn't know who I really was. She's doing fine and will be going to live with her sister when she's discharged. What she told me was...' she hesitated for a moment, 'illuminating.'

'In what way?' Thea asked.

'It turns out that Miriam and Victor were *engaged* to be married.'

'What?' Thea halted and grabbed hold of her sister's arm, bringing her to a standstill so she could speak to her face to face. 'But he couldn't be engaged to her when he was already married to you!'

'Victor dismissed that fact. He'd lied to Miriam, telling her he was a lonely bachelor living in Wykeham, so had no children but did have a dragon of a housekeeper called Prudence.' Prue's eyes hardened. 'He deceived Miriam and she believed everything he told her. There was no reason why she should think otherwise.'

'The lying... even telling her you were his *dragon of a housekeeper*! How dare he?' Thea shook her head. 'It was even worse than you thought. Did you tell her the truth?'

Prue looked off into the distance for a moment before returning her gaze to meet Thea's. 'No, I didn't. I took pity on the woman. She's hurt enough. My revealing how badly she had been lied to wouldn't help her, would it? It would just make her feel even worse and I couldn't do that to her.'

'Oh Prue!' Thea put her arms around her sister and held her tightly. 'That was such a kind thing to do.' When they'd let go of each other, she added, 'You know there are few women who'd have been so compassionate.'

Prue gave a small shrug. 'I think Miriam is as much a victim of Victor's rotten behaviour as I am. She seems a genuine, decent woman and I'm pretty sure if she'd known the truth, then she wouldn't have touched Victor with the proverbial barge pole.'

'I never liked him and I dislike him even more now,' Thea said, thinking that Victor had sunk to even lower depths than she'd thought possible. 'What about you? How do you feel after finding all that out?'

Prue gave a sad smile. 'It's helped me. Before I spoke to Miriam I blamed her as well as him, but now...' she threw a hand out wide. 'I know different. It's all Victor's doing and he's gone. I can't change the past, but I do have a new future and one he isn't involved in. It feels such a relief.' Tears filled Prue's eyes, highlighting their blueness.

Thea grabbed her sister's hand. 'You'll have a wonderful future, Prue. I wish you so much happiness.'

'Thank you. I know things won't always run smoothly but that heavy cloud that's hung over me since I married him is gone.' She smiled tentatively. 'I'm free!'

Thea returned Prue's smile, noticing the way her sister was standing tall, looking strong and determined. In time, once all this was settled, there was a good chance that Prue would be fine — and probably better than ever.

CHAPTER 28

Hettie read the letter that had just arrived for her in the afternoon post and let out a squeal of delight.

'Is everything all right?' Marianne asked, swaying from side to side as she cradled baby Bea in her arms. The little girl was fractious and grizzly with a tooth coming through and wouldn't go down for a nap like her sister was now having.

'My great-niece Lucille is coming to visit. She's got some leave and will be here on Saturday,' Hettie said. 'That's something lovely to look forward to.'

The past few days since the last raid on Norwich and Victor's death had been difficult ones. Although Hettie hadn't thought well of Victor, his sudden demise was still a shock and ripples from it had spread outwards, affecting not only Prue and her children, but the wider family and local community too. The people of Great Plumstead had been stunned to hear what had happened, but of course they didn't know the real reason Victor had been in Norwich and who he'd been with. Prue was having to deal with everything while hiding the truth about her late husband's adulterous behaviour.

'After tomorrow's funeral, hopefully things will settle down again,' Hettie said. 'Lucille's visit will give us a much-needed boost and distraction. I'm looking forward to hearing about her work in London and life in Canada.'

'Prue's doing so well,' Marianne said. 'She did a shift at The Mother's Day Club this morning and hasn't let what's happened slow her down.'

'You know Prue – she likes to keep busy.' Hettie checked the time on the clock standing on the kitchen dresser. 'If I go now, then I'll be able to catch Ada and tell her about Lucille's visit and still be back in time to finish making the tea. The casserole's already cooking in the slow oven so that should be fine.'

'It's a lovely day for a bike ride.' Marianne shifted Bea in her arms as she looked out of the kitchen window where the May afternoon was bathed in sunlight.

'It certainly is. May's my favourite month of the year. I love how everything's so fresh looking, green and growing. I'd better stop talking and get going. I'll see you later.'

Hettie folded Lucille's letter and placed it in her handbag, then went into the scullery where she put on her hat, checking in the mirror that it was straight before heading out to fetch her bicycle. It was such a pleasure to venture outside now without a coat on as the weather was warming up. Her blue knitted cardigan over her dress was enough for today.

Pedalling along the long, tree-lined drive leading to Great Plumstead Hall, Hettie marvelled at the glorious, newly unfurled pale-green beech leaves overhead. They created a soft green cathedral-like roof, which was breathtakingly beautiful. Hettie had seen it many times before, during her time working at the Hall, but she never tired of it. The sight of it always made her heart sing, along with the view of the carpet of bluebells stretching off into the woods on the right. A gentle breeze carried their subtle scent towards her and Hettie breathed in deeply. Today was turning out better than she'd expected, what with Lucille's letter and now her impromptu visit to see Ada and the chance to immerse herself in the heavenly sights and smells of springtime.

Hettie expected her sister would be as enthusiastic about Lucille's visit as she was. Ada had been curious when Hettie had shown her Lucille's first letter back in February, keen to know more. As befitting the oldest sister, Ada had bossed Hettie and her two brothers around when they were young, especially after their mother died and Ada had returned home to look after her father and siblings. Hettie remembered how upset Ada had been when their brothers emigrated to Canada; although she'd not shown it outwardly, Hettie could tell how she felt. Ada had missed them as much as Hettie did. Having a granddaughter of their brother Sidney come to see them would be a most welcome connection with him after all these years.

Reaching the end of the drive, Hettie steered her bicycle across the wide sweep of gravel in front of the honey-coloured building towards the west wing where Ada was the housekeeper. The owners, Lord and Lady Campbell-Gryce, had moved into the smaller wing when the Hall was converted into a hospital for the duration of the war.

Parking her bicycle, Hettie headed for the back door into the servants' area where she was likely to find her sister. As Hettie entered the kitchen, Dorothy Shepherd, the cook, looked up from her work rolling out pastry on a marble slab.

'This is a lovely surprise,' Dorothy said, giving Hettie a welcoming wave. 'Will you join me for a cup of tea once this is finished? And there's some freshly baked scones as well.'

'Hello, Dorothy. Yes please, I'd love some tea and a scone and a good catch-up. I was hoping to speak to Ada as well.'

'She's taken a tray of tea things to her Ladyship; she'll be back soon. Is everything all right?' Dorothy asked.

'Yes, I've got some good news...' She halted as her sister appeared in the doorway.

'Hettie, what are you doing here?' Ada asked, advancing into the kitchen.

'I've come to tell you that our great-niece Lucille is coming to visit. She's arriving on Saturday,' Hettie announced. 'Isn't that wonderful? Just what we need right now.'

Ada nodded happily. 'It is. You must bring her here for afternoon tea. We can arrange something nice for her, can't we, Dorothy? Show how we do things at the Hall. I don't suppose they have places like this in Canada.'

'Of course we can,' Dorothy agreed.

Hettie suppressed a chuckle, thinking how much Ada loved living here at Great Plumstead Hall and would enjoy showing it off to Lucille. 'I'm sure she'd like that very much, thank you.'

'I'll make us some tea and you can tell us about the details for tomorrow,' Ada said, motioning for Hettie to take a seat at the large wooden table.

'The funeral's at two o'clock and there's tea and sandwiches afterwards at the village hall. Jack and Alice are arriving home tonight. They've both been given seventy-two hour passes so it will be a short visit but enough to be there for Prue and to see their father buried,' Hettie explained.

'How is Prue?' Dorothy asked, gently lowering a circle of pastry into a pie dish.

'She's keeping herself busy, which helps. There's been a lot to arrange and there'll be more to sort out after the funeral, what with Victor's business in Wykeham,' Hettie said.

'It must have been a terrible shock for her,' Dorothy said, laying slices of apple into the pie dish.

Hettie nodded, thinking the shock was as much where Victor had been killed and why he was there, but then most people like Dorothy didn't know that. 'It was,' she said, wishing the truth could be told but knowing that for the sake of Prue and her children it never could.

'Well I won't be going to Norwich again until this war is over,' Ada declared, putting the freshly made pot of tea and a plate of scones on the table. 'It's far safer here in Great Plumstead.'

'Bombs can fall anywhere,' Hettie reminded her.

'Maybe, but I don't think this village is on Hitler's target list, unlike places like Norwich or London,' Ada retorted, setting out cups on the table. 'So there's less chance of having a bomb fall on me!'

Hettie met Dorothy's eye and a look of amusement passed between them.

'Fair enough,' Hettie said. 'Now, what day's best for me to bring Lucille to visit you? She's arriving on Saturday and leaving the following Friday.'

Ada considered for a moment before saying at last, 'On Sunday. It's my afternoon off so I won't be on duty. We'll have tea and cake and then I can show her around.' She gave a smile. 'I shall look forward to it.'

CHAPTER 29

Prue stared at her reflection in the mirror. The black dress she wore might look the part, but inside she was anything but a grieving widow. In the days since Victor's death and then her visit to see Miriam Roper at the hospital, Prue's thoughts had had time to settle. It was as if she'd been in a thick fog dealing with the aftermath and the shocking discovery of the extent of her husband's lies and deception to both his family and his mistress.

Now the simple truth was Prue felt relieved that he was gone. Victor's dominant presence had loomed over her since they'd married and although in recent years she'd begun to make some progress in standing her ground against him, he'd still had a huge negative effect on her life.

Before he'd been killed, she'd been planning how to break free knowing it wouldn't be easy and there would have been consequences for her and others.

Prue let out a sigh. At least Victor's death had removed the problem of having to tell him she wanted a divorce and the need to leave her home. But her feelings must be kept private

ROSIE HENDRY

because today was about the final scene in her sham of a marriage – Victor's funeral.

As Victor was a seemingly respectable member of the community and businessman, sitting on numerous committees and even part of the village Home Guard, Prue expected there to be a large turnout this afternoon. People would come to show their respects to the man they *thought* they'd known. If only they knew the truth about Victor. The way he behaved at home. The lies he told and the mistress he had. What would they say if they discovered he'd been killed while he was at his mistress's house? And that he was *engaged* to her, even though he already had a wife?

Prue shook her head to rid herself of these thoughts because they would never know. Could never know. Although it irritated her because she would love the truth to be known, it was better to let it go. News like that would be scandalous and the gossips would never forget. It was better that Prue be seen as a widow with her husband killed in an air raid in Norwich, than one whose husband had died while he was with his other woman. She didn't want that scandal to tar Alice, Jack or Edwin either.

No, today was about going through a performance – the custom of sending off the departed in the time-honoured tradition. Prue would play her role and focus on the future. It was what she did in the coming weeks, months and years that was important. Victor would be buried and then she could move on.

A gentle tap on the bedroom door brought Prue's thoughts firmly back to the present.

'Ma, are you ready?' Jack stepped into the room, looking smart in his army uniform. 'Are you all right?'

She nodded. 'Yes, I'm fine. Let's get this over with, shall we?'

146

His eyes met hers, a look of understanding passing between them. Although Jack knew nothing about Victor's mistress and never would from Prue, he understood all too well that his parents' marriage had not been a happy one. He'd been witness to how Victor had behaved from the start.

'How are you?' she asked, brushing a piece of fluff off the shoulder of his uniform tunic.

'I'm fine.' He gave her a small, tentative smile. 'But I'll be better when today's done.'

Prue stood on tiptoes and kissed his cheek. 'We all will. In a few hour's time it will all be over.'

The church was full and from where Prue sat in the front pew, with Jack and Alice on either side of her, she could feel the presence of people packed into the rows behind her. Her family – Thea, Reuben, Lizzie plus Hettie – were in the pew immediately behind and she welcomed their support, especially as some of them knew the truth.

Many of the mourners' faces had been full of sympathy for Prue and her children as they'd walked down the aisle to take their seats. She could imagine their thoughts, that here was a family devastated by the sudden shock of Victor's death at the hands of enemy bombers.

Prue turned her attention to the coffin standing in front of the altar to the left of her, the rector's words blurring into a fuzzy noise in her ears. It was hard to believe that Victor lay inside it. His fiery temper, dominating ways and his narrow-mindedness all silenced and stilled for ever. He would no longer spoil the joy in their home or have her walking on eggshells around him for fear of sparking some rebuke or one-sided argument.

Enough, Prue told herself, firmly. Victor is gone and you're free. Instead, she moved her focus to the flowers lying on top of the coffin, which she'd picked this morning. She let the sight of them carry her out of the church and to her garden, escaping in her mind while her body remained playing its role. Prue imagined herself strolling around her lawn in summer sunshine, smelling the fragrant roses and sweet peas, listening to the chatter of the swallows flying overhead and cheeps of sparrows in the house eaves. It calmed and soothed her.

It was only when Jack placed his hand on Prue's arm that she allowed herself to become fully present again. She looked at her son, who with a small tilt of his head signalled for her to stand. The service was over and the pall bearers were lifting Victor's coffin onto their shoulders for his last journey to his resting place in the churchyard.

Prue turned to Alice, standing on the other side, who'd remained silent throughout the service, not even joining in with singing any of the hymns.

'Are you all right?' Prue asked.

Alice gave her a small but unconvincing smile.

Prue linked her arm through Alice's. 'It's nearly over now,' she said in a low voice, concerned about her daughter and wishing this was over so she could take her home. 'I know it's not easy – you're doing so well.'

Keeping their arms linked to support Alice, who looked pale, Prue followed Jack out into the aisle and, walking with her children on either side, they joined the coffin's procession towards the church door.

Walking slowly, Prue could see more of the mourners than she had on the way in. An air force blue uniform caught her eye and she saw that Patsy, the Waaf who'd stayed with them, was there. The young woman gave a nod of her head and Prue returned it, thankful Patsy had come here today to support them.

Outside it was an overcast day, the grey clouds having rolled in last night following a few days of glorious spring sunshine. It was appropriate funeral weather, Prue mused as they followed the coffin through the churchyard to the prepared grave. Reaching the graveside, the pall bearers placed the coffin on to the ropes, ready for it to be lowered into the earth. The vicar waited as the rest of the mourners arrived from the church and then the committal part of the service began.

As the vicar recited the age-old words, Prue heard sniffing and glanced at Alice standing beside her, who was blotting her eyes with her handkerchief. Prue immediately put her arm around her daughter and pulled her close. Despite how badly Victor had behaved, soft-hearted Alice still loved him. Looking to her left, Prue saw Jack standing stony-faced, his own opinion of his father less favourable, especially after the appalling way Victor had treated his brother.

Prue's thoughts flew to Edwin, who was serving with the Friends' Ambulance Unit and had been unable to travel the long distance back from North Africa. That was probably a good thing, Prue thought, because after Victor's callous behaviour towards his younger son for being a conscientious objector, he didn't deserve to have him at his funeral. Edwin had sent Prue a thoughtful and caring telegram in response to hers informing him of Victor's death. She knew a letter from Edwin would be following soon, the young man was bound to want to say more to help Prue as well as he could from afar.

When at last the service was over, Prue was relieved to be able to lead Alice from the graveside hoping her daughter would start to feel better once they were away from the oppressive feel of the funeral service and burial. It was only a short walk to the village hall where there would be some refreshments on offer. Gloria and other members from The Mother's Day Club had volunteered to organise it for her: just simple cups of tea and sandwiches for any mourners who wanted to join them.

Entering the hall, Prue found herself wrapped in a perfumy embrace as Gloria threw both her arms around her and hugged her tightly.

'You all right, ducks?' Gloria asked, stepping back.

'Yes, I'm glad it's over,' Prue said, grateful for her friend's support. 'Thank you for organising everything here.' She looked around the hall where tables had been put up near the doorway to the kitchen, set out with plates of food and cups ready by the large tea urn. Other members of The Mother's Day Club stood behind tables, waiting to serve. 'It looks perfect. I'm not sure how many will come. There were a lot at the church.'

'Don't you worry about a thing. Alice, you take your mother to get some tea and I'll mind the door and direct people in,' Gloria instructed, heading for the doorway where people had started to arrive.

'Come on, Ma,' Alice said, who was looking a bit better now the funeral service and burial was over. 'Let Gloria work her charm.'

Prue allowed her daughter to lead the way, pleased to have a chance to gather her thoughts and energy with a cup of tea before she had to carry out the last part of today's performance – talking to the many mourners.

'How are you feeling?' Prue asked her daughter after they'd got themselves some tea and moved to stand in a quiet corner of the hall.

'A bit better. Funerals are so...' Alice frowned. 'I just wanted it to be over with. I never imagined my first trip home from the WAAF would be to go to Father's funeral.' Her eyes filled with tears.

Prue pulled her daughter into a one armed-hug and Alice rested her head on her mother's shoulder. 'It will soon be done and we can go home.'

'He didn't even say goodbye to me the day I left to join the WAAF,' Alice said in a hushed voice.

Prue recalled that morning at breakfast when Victor had displayed his self-centred behaviour not wishing his daughter well, or even just a courteous goodbye before he left for work. Now he would never get the chance to do so. Clearly it had hurt Alice. 'I remember. He shouldn't have done that.'

Alice took a deep breath and raised her head. 'I'm glad I've got you, Ma.'

'I'm always here for you,' Prue said. 'Anytime you need me you just let me know, all right?'

Alice nodded. 'Thank you, I promise I will.' She put her cup of tea on a nearby table. 'I think I'll go and freshen up in the ladies.'

Prue watched her daughter make her way through the throng of mourners hoping that in time Alice would recover from the shock of her father's sudden death and his unsupportive treatment of her brave decision to volunteer to join the WAAF. Whatever happened, Prue would always be immensely proud of Alice, just as she was of Jack and Edwin.

She took a mouthful of tea and felt her stomach knot at the sight of Victor's brother, Claude, descending on her. She had seen he was at the funeral but had avoided talking to him until now.

'Prudence,' Claude said in his oily voice as he approached her. 'What a sad day it is!'

'Hello Claude.' She forced the words out, doing her best not to show the revulsion she felt on seeing him and hearing him use her full name, just like his brother had. Victor had been horrible enough, but his younger brother was equally abhorrent at best. The pair of them shared the same icy blue eyes and arrogant manner, believing their way was the right way about everything. Thankfully Claude had never married so no woman had ever had to put up with him.

Over the years Prue had rarely seen Claude, something she was thankful for, but she knew Victor kept in regular touch with him and they'd met up from time to time. The fact that Victor's father had left the agricultural merchant's business to Victor and not shared it between both of his sons had rankled Claude. It didn't matter that Claude had been left a tidy lump sum instead, which he'd used to start his own now very successful business in another market town, he still hankered for what his older brother had got. Was that why he was sniffing around now? Prue wondered. Was he hoping that at last the business would come to him?

'Poor old Victor. He never thought he'd end up cut off in his prime by an enemy bomb.' Claude shook his head. 'And while doing his civic duty too. I warned him he was taking on too much committee stuff, meetings for this and meetings for that.' He pursed his lips into a thin line. 'He should have been putting that time into his business, not minding other people's, because that won't get you anywhere.'

'No, well, I'm sure he didn't expect it,' Prue said, wondering how quickly she could extricate herself from him.

'Take me for example, in my opinion the best way we can help with this war is to keep our businesses running smoothly because they oil the workings of the local community, provide the shops where people can buy what they need...' Prue tuned out of what Claude was saying and was relieved when Mr Jefferson, Victor's solicitor, caught her eye. She must have conveyed a sense of needing help as he immediately approached her.

'I'm sorry to interrupt, but I need to speak to you Mrs Wilson, before I return to my office in Wykeham,' Mr Jefferson said. 'Please excuse us.' He put his hand on Prue's elbow and steered her over to a quiet corner of the hall, which had filled up with mourners in the past few minutes and was becoming loud with conversation.

'Thank you for coming to my rescue,' Prue said appreciatively.

Mr Jefferson gave her a knowing smile. 'You're welcome. I could see you were cornered there. I have experience with Mr Claude Wilson from when your late husband's father died and I performed the reading of the will.' He cleared his throat. 'It's Victor's will that I wanted to talk to you about. I would be obliged if Mr Jack Wilson and Miss Alice Wilson could be there when it's read as well as yourself.'

'They're both only home for a short while before they have to return to the army and WAAF,' Prue said. 'Tomorrow is the only day they could come.'

'Then tomorrow it shall be. Shall we say eleven o'clock?' Mr Jefferson suggested.

'That would be fine.'

'I will see you then. Please accept my deepest condolences for your loss.'

Prue nodded. 'Thank you.'

'Now if you'll excuse me, I really must return to my office. Until tomorrow.' He bowed his head and turned to go, weaving his way through the gathered mourners.

'How are you doing?' a voice asked and Prue turned to see her sister Lizzie standing beside her.

'All right.' Prue lowered her voice. 'But I'll be glad when this is over and I can go home.'

'I saw you were being spoken at by Claude,' Lizzie said, her eyes drifting to where he was now in conversation with Ernie Davies, the deputy manager of Victor's shop. 'What's he up to?'

'Who knows, but I have a horrible feeling we haven't seen the last of him.'

'Nasty slimy, smarmy man!' Lizzie gave a shudder. 'What would he say if he knew...' Her voice tailed off as her eyes met Prue's, the meaning of her unspoken words clear.

'I think he'd have thought Victor would have been better putting his time into the business and making more money than messing about with...,' Prue said in a hushed voice, leaning closer to her sister so only she could hear. 'Claude's number one things in life are pounds, shillings and pence. Victor was bad enough about valuing them too highly, but his brother is ten times worse.'

'Drink up your tea and I'll get you something to eat. I daresay you haven't had much today.' Lizzie looked around her and, spotting Hettie and Thea, beckoned them over. 'But I'll leave you in Hettie and Thea's care, so you don't get trapped again.' She turned to her oldest sister, 'You'll keep a watch over Prue, won't you?'

'Of course we will,' Thea assured her.

'You've had enough to deal with today without any more nonsense,' Hettie added, flicking her eyes in Claude's direction. He was now waving his arms around as he vented forth about something to Ernie Davies, who looked like he wanted to escape.

'Thank you.' Prue gave them all a grateful smile. She was so glad of their unstinting support. Having them all by her side was making a tough day a lot easier.

CHAPTER 30

'First of all, my sincere condolences to you all for your loss,' Mr Jefferson began, peering at them over his half-moon glasses across his leather-topped desk. 'Thank you for coming here today, particularly as I understand your leave ends tomorrow.' He directed this last comment to Jack and Alice, who sat either side of Prue facing the white-haired solicitor.

'Thank you for seeing us at such short notice.' Prue gave him a warm smile. She liked Mr Jefferson, who had an air of solid reliability and decency about him.

'To business then.' The solicitor picked up the document in front of him, cleared his throat and began to read aloud. 'This is the last will and testament of I, Victor Charles Wilson, and I revoke all former wills…'

Prue could almost hear Victor's voice saying the words and an icy shiver crept down her spine.

'I give and bequeath to my wife, Prudence Anne Wilson the sum of one hundred pounds. To my daughter Alice Catherine Wilson, the sum of one thousand pounds.' Mr Jefferson continued and Prue felt as if the air had been sucked out of the room. 'To my son Jack Victor Wilson, I leave my house at Mill Lane in Great Plumstead, my business, Wilson's Seed and Agricultural Merchants and the contents of savings accounts...'

Mr Jefferson finished reading the will, but there was no mention of any further bequests. There was nothing for Edwin.

The room was silent for a few moments before Jack jumped to his feet declaring, 'Father can't do that! How could he leave so little to Ma and Alice and cut my brother out completely?'

Prue grabbed hold of his hand. 'Sit down, Jack! Getting angry won't help.' She was as shaken by the severity of Victor's last will and testament as her son was. Although she and Victor had never discussed his intentions, she'd never imagined he would do this. It felt like he was still dominating their lives from beyond the grave. Would she ever be free of him?

'I appreciate that the contents of Victor's will must have come as a shock to you.' Mr Jefferson tapped his finger on the document now laid on the desk in front of him. 'I can tell you he had the will rewritten two years ago and made significant changes to it. But I'm afraid I am not at liberty to say exactly what those were.'

'You mean he cut Edwin out of it,' Jack said, now sitting back in his chair. 'Well, I'm not sticking to what Father wanted. He might have left everything to me, bar one thousand pounds to Alice and one hundred pounds to Ma, but I'm changing that. I want Ma to have all he left to me. It's what she deserves and is right, the business and house, everything!'

'Jack, you mustn't do that,' Prue said, putting a hand on his arm. 'Your father inherited the business from his father, and his before him.'

'Well, *I don't want it*, especially at the expense of the rest of my family. I never want to work there again.' Jack fixed his gaze on Prue, his blue eyes earnest. 'If I survive the war, then I'm going to be an engineer. What do you think, Alice?'

'I agree that Ma should have been left the house and business,' Alice said firmly.

'But you might change your mind, Jack,' Prue warned him. 'Having a business would set you up for life and if you still didn't want it in a few years' time, then you could sell it and use the money to start an engineering firm instead.'

'No Ma, I can't! And I won't. It's not fair to you all,' Jack said adamantly.

'Can I make a suggestion?' Mr Jefferson asked.

'Of course,' Prue said.

'Jack could share the business between the four of you – Alice, Edwin, Jack and yourself, Mrs Wilson. A quarter each,' Mr Jefferson said.

Jack thought for a moment and then said, 'That I would accept. But I want Ma to have the house and money. It's her home and it should be hers now.'

'I'd rather not have the one hundred pounds Victor left me and have the money equally divided between all of us, the same as with the business and the house. It's our family home,' Prue said.

'But I want you to be secure, Ma. To have the house in your name so you'll always have a home,' Jack said. 'I'll agree to dividing the business and money fairly between us.'

Prue considered this for a moment. 'Very well. Mr Jefferson can we make sure that the house will be left to Jack, Edwin and Alice equally after my death so they have their share then?'

'Yes, I can do that,' the solicitor agreed, making a note. 'Can

I ask who will be doing the day to day running of the business?'

'I don't have the time or inclination to do that,' Prue admitted.

'I understand Victor's deputy manager Ernie Davies is very capable and trustworthy,' Mr Jefferson said. 'He might be willing to take over the role of manager for you.'

'Ernie's a good man,' Jack said. 'I'll speak to him about it but I'm sure he'd be interested, especially if we increase his wages to match the added responsibility. Will you organise things for me, Mr Jefferson, please? The transfer of the house to Ma and ownership of the business and money equally between me, Edwin, Alice and Ma.'

The solicitor nodded. 'I can, providing you're sure it's what you want. You'll be giving up a lot. You could be set up for life, you know.'

'I'm sure,' Jack said firmly. 'It's what I want.'

'And Miss Wilson, are you in agreement?' Mr Jefferson asked, peering at Alice over his glasses.

Alice nodded. 'I am. Father might have left me money, but he was very unfair to Edwin and Ma. I want the same as Ma, to not have my one thousand pounds but instead to share things equally between the four of us, except the house. That will make things fairer and more secure for the future for all of us and especially Ma.' She glanced at Prue and gave her a loving smile.

'Very well, as you're all agreed. Victor's will must go through probate first, but then I can do as you ask.' Mr Jefferson picked up his pen and made a few quick notes. 'Mr Wilson and Miss Wilson, if you would both leave your address with my secretary, I'll be in touch with you and begin the process of following your wishes.' He looked thoughtful.

'You're a very generous young man. Not many would do as you want to.'

'I wish my father had had the decency to do the right thing by his wife and *all* his children,' Jack said bitterly. 'Thank you for your help.'

'I'm glad to be of service.' The solicitor stood up and walked around his desk, signalling the end of their meeting. He held out his hand for each of them to shake.

'Thank you,' Prue said as she shook hands, the older man giving her a look of sympathy.

'I'll be in touch.' Mr Jefferson walked to the door and opened it for them. 'Good day to you and take care.'

As they stepped outside into Wykeham marketplace, Prue still felt shocked by the stunning revelations inside the solicitor's office and the severity of Victor's last will towards her and their children. It wasn't that surprising that Victor had left the business only to Jack, just as Victor's father had to him. However to cut out Edwin completely and to bequeath her only one hundred pounds after so many years of marriage was like a slap in the face and a sign of how little he thought of her. But then hadn't Victor told her he'd only married her to look after the house and children? She was cheaper than having to pay the wages of a housekeeper or nanny. Interestingly Victor had made no bequest to Miriam Roper either, although Prue wouldn't mention that to her children.

'Are you all right, Ma?' Jack said.

She looked up at him, noting his worried face, and forced a small smile. 'I'm shocked, but I shouldn't be, knowing your father.'

Jack rubbed the back of his neck. '*He* might have been like that, but I'm not. With Mr Jefferson's help we can put things right and just as they should have been.' He put his arm around Prue. 'Don't worry, Ma, we'll get it sorted. Will you write and tell Edwin what's going on for me? You know I'm not much of a one for writing letters.'

'Of course.' Prue leaned her head against Jack's shoulder for a moment. 'You really are a generous soul, Jack.'

'My family is important to me and so is fairness,' he said. 'I'm going to have a word with Ernie Davies. See if he's willing to become manager.'

'How about we have a cup of tea in a teashop, Ma, my treat?' Alice said. 'Maybe even a nice cake if they've got any. We could do with something after that meeting, don't you think?'

Prue took her daughter's hand and squeezed it. 'I agree, and shall we get something for you too, Jack? You could join us in a short while.'

'All right then,' he agreed. 'I'll make it a quick meeting if there's a chance of some tea and cake on offer.' Jack grinned and bent down to kiss Prue's cheek. 'I'll see you soon.'

Prue watched her son walk across the marketplace to where Victor's business, the seed and agricultural merchants, stood on the far side. How different he was from his father. She was proud of the man Jack had grown into, one who valued his family far more than wealth and business.

As she and Alice walked towards the teashop, Prue wondered what Victor would have said about Jack's decision. He would never have understood the motivation behind it and definitely would not have approved. But Victor was gone and despite his attempt to push their family in the direction *he* wanted it to go, his wishes had been thwarted by his son's caring nature. Jack was so much more of a decent man than his father was, there wasn't even a hint of Victor's ways or personality in him.

CHAPTER 31

It was Saturday morning and to make up for lost time earlier in the week while they attended the funeral, Thea, Flo and Nancy were busy hoeing to keep on top of the weeds, which were growing rapidly with the warmer spring weather. It was a necessary but tedious job which was always made better with company, Thea thought, cutting through some chickweed.

'How's Prue?' Flo asked, directing her question to Nancy.

'All right, I think. She was sad to see Jack and Alice leave, but she's keeping busy. She was going to work out the first rota for the Rural Pie Scheme this morning, ready for it to start next week,' Nancy said as she worked. 'There are plenty of volunteers to 'elp deliver the pies so I 'ope it works out well.'

'I'm sure Prue's got it well organised, and it will help keep her mind off things as well,' Thea said.

Thea was worried about Prue. Despite her outward appearance of coping well, Thea had a feeling that deep down her sister was still reeling from the shock of Victor's unexpected death at his mistress's house, followed by Miriam's revelation that they were engaged. On top of which had come the shocking reading of Victor's will, the details of which Prue had told Thea about while they were out in the WVS canteen yesterday. It was a lot to deal with and even though Prue's marriage hadn't been a happy one, the depth of Victor's lies had been appalling.

The sound of children's voices interrupted Thea's thoughts, and she stopped hoeing and turned to see George and Betty, along with Nancy's two daughters Marie and Joan, running in the gate of Five Acres field towards them.

'Can we play in the Anderson shelter please, Auntie Thea?' Betty called. 'Marie and Joan haven't got one at their house and we thought we could play air raids.'

'All right then, but don't light any of the candles in there,' Thea told them. 'You'll just have to keep the door open a bit so you can see.'

'We'll be careful,' George said.

The children turned on their heels and ran off to the Anderson shelter nearer the house.

'Imagine wanting to play air raids,' Nancy said, shaking her head. 'That ain't a game we played when we were young, but to these children being brought up in wartime, it's them mimicking what they see.'

'Living in wartime affects them as much as grown-ups,' Flo said, working nearby. 'All four of them have been taken away from their homes because of the war. It's deprived them of having the normal childhood they should have had.'

'But they're happy,' Thea said. 'They've adapted and settled.'

'Very true,' Nancy agreed, jabbing at a weed with her hoe. 'We might 'ave 'ad to leave our 'omes in London, but we 'ave all gained a lot from living in the countryside too. Seen and done things we would never 'ave experienced otherwise.'

'We'll pop in and have a look at their air-raid game when we've done here,' Thea said. 'Then there are some more beans to sow and beetroot, too. Plenty to keep us busy today!'

CHAPTER 32

Hettie stood on the platform of Great Plumstead station waiting for Lucille's train to arrive, her mind drifting back to the day she'd last seen her two brothers at this same place. It was in the spring of 1900 after Sidney and Albert had made the life-changing decision to emigrate to Canada. They'd spent months talking about it, reading anything they could lay their hands on about their future home, and had finally booked their passage across the Atlantic and were off.

Her brothers had asked Hettie to go with them to Canada but she'd declined. Then, aged twenty-one, she had risen from her starting position as a scullery maid at the Hall and was working as a kitchen maid with her eye on becoming a cook one day. She was gaining experience, learning so much, and wasn't prepared to give it up for the risky notion of moving to a new country thousands of miles from home.

Sidney and Albert wanted adventure and to experience a new land, where they believed they'd have a greater chance of doing better for themselves than if they stayed working as farm labourers. It had been a gamble but it had paid off. Both of her brothers had done well, setting up in business together, each marrying and having families.

Hettie was glad it had worked out for them, the only sadness being that she hadn't seen them since the day she'd waved them off all those years ago. But now, she could see smoke from the approaching train — Sidney's granddaughter was on her way to where he'd started from, coming full circle. Hettie was brimming over with happiness at the thought of meeting Lucille and reconnecting that link with her brothers, no matter that it was two generations down.

She watched as the train came steaming into the station and halted alongside the platform. As the passengers disembarked, she didn't know which of the women dressed in the air force blue uniform was Lucille. Most of them seemed to know where they were going as they walked towards the exit, bound for the aerodrome, leaving a young woman carrying a suitcase standing on the platform. Grinning broadly, she headed towards Hettie.

'Aunt Hettie?' she asked in a Canadian accent that sounded so different from the local voices.

'Yes, that's me! Welcome to Great Plumstead, Lucille.' Hettie beamed and held her arms open wide. 'Come here and let me give you a hug.'

Lucille put her suitcase down and went into Hettie's arms, returning the embrace.

'I'm so glad you're here.' Hettie stepped back and stared up at her great-niece, who was far taller than she was. 'Let me get a good look at you.' The young woman was striking looking with eyes the colour of forget-me-nots, creamy pale skin and dark glossy hair under her air force cap. 'I can hardly believe Sidney's granddaughter is here. Before you arrived, I was thinking back to the day I waved him and Albert off from this very station. To have you come and stay makes me so happy.'

'Grandpa was delighted when I wrote and told him I was coming to visit. He's sent me something to give you,' Lucille said. 'He wishes he could have come too.'

'You'll be able to write and tell him all about it.' Hettie put her arm through Lucille's. 'Let's get you home to Rookery House and settled. There's lots to tell and show you but there's no rush. You're on your holiday so don't want to overdo things.'

'I appreciate you having me stay,' Lucille said as they fell into step with each other and left the station. 'It feels good to have family here in England to visit. I'm real excited about seeing where Grandpa lived when he was a boy and meeting Aunt Ada.'

'Ada's looking forward to meeting you, too,' Hettie said. 'I'll take you to see her tomorrow.'

'I hope you'll be comfortable in here.' Hettie cast her eye around the dining room where a camp bed had been set up for Lucille to sleep on. Hettie had made it look bright and cheerful by putting a colourful patchwork-covered eiderdown on the top. 'I'm sorry we don't have a proper bedroom to give you, only they're all occupied.'

'It's perfect. I'll be comfortable in here and having a room all to myself is such a luxury. I've never had one before, always sharing with my sisters, then lots of other women when I joined up. Even in London, I have to share with two other girls. Now let me find Grandpa's gift for you.'

Lucille opened her suitcase, took out a large envelope and handed it to Hettie. 'I hope you like it.'

Wondering what was inside, Hettie opened it and pulled

out three photographs. Her eyes were immediately drawn to the man sitting in the front row of the group of gathered people in the first picture. She recognised him at once. He might be much older than when Hettie last saw him, but there was no doubting that smile. It was her brother Sidney.

'Oh my goodness!' She put her hand to her mouth as tears filled her eyes.

'Grandpa thought you might like to see him and Grandma and all our family. This is my Pa and Ma…' Lucille pointed to them and told Hettie the name of each person in the photo. 'And there's me,' she ended.

'All these people coming from Sidney going to Canada,' Hettie said, staring at the photograph.

'There's more. Look at the next photograph,' Lucille said.

Moving on to the second one, Hettie spotted her other brother Albert, with his family gathered around him. Again Lucille pointed out and named everyone. They were names Hettie knew from her brothers' letters and now she had a chance to put faces to them.

'Take a look at the last photo,' Lucille said.

Hettie smiled as she selected the one which showed the two brothers and their families combined. Brothers, husbands, wives, sons, daughters and cousins, each one there because Sidney and Albert took the risk of changing their lives to start again in a new country. Hettie was delighted at how their lives had turned out for them.

'When were these taken?' Hettie asked.

'On Grandpa's birthday last year. They had a big party for him and invited the whole family, and for once, they all managed to be there,' Lucille said. 'That wouldn't be possible now with me over here, and my brother and some of my cousins serving overseas too.'

'I'll treasure these and will write and thank Sidney tonight.'

Hettie took a last look before replacing them safely in the envelope. 'We must show them to Ada.'

'No need. Grandpa sent her copies too.' Lucille took out another envelope from the case. 'He thought it best.'

Hettie let out a laugh. 'Very wise. He knows Ada well and she would be most put out if I'd been given photographs and she hadn't. Thank you for bringing them to me.' She laid her hand on Lucille's arm. 'Now I have some freshly baked Norfolk shortcakes you might like.'

'That sounds wonderful,' Lucille said. 'I love trying different English foods, though I'm less keen on some than others. We were served some tripe in the canteen last week and I didn't like that!'

Settled at the kitchen table, Lucille took a bite of Norfolk shortcake and chewed slowly, a look of pleasure spreading across her face.

'That's delicious, Aunt Hettie,' she said after swallowing her mouthful. 'Far, far better than tripe!'

Hettie laughed. 'I'm glad to hear it. It was one of Sidney's favourites when he was a boy.' She poured them both a cup of tea and had just helped herself to a shortcake when there was a knock on the kitchen door; it opened and Elspeth stepped inside, followed by Marge.

'Hello Hettie, we've...' Elspeth halted at the sight of Lucille. 'Oh, I'm sorry. We didn't realise you had company.'

'Come on in and sit down.' Hettie got to her feet. 'This is my niece Lucille who's in the Canadian air force and visiting from London. Lucille, this is Elspeth and Marge who work on the local aerodrome. They stayed here for a couple of weeks earlier this year until their accommodation was ready.'

While Hettie fetched more cups and plates, she smiled to

herself as she watched the young women greeting each other and it wasn't long before they were swapping stories and comparing life in the Canadian and British air forces. What a joy it was to have these young, vibrant women in her life, Hettie thought. She was going to enjoy Lucille's visit very much indeed.

CHAPTER 33

Prue was working in the vegetable plot in her garden, pushing hazel twigs into the soil for the pea plants to climb up, when she felt prickles on the back of her neck and knew she was not alone. She whipped around to discover Victor's brother Claude watching her from near the house. Prue's heart plummeted. What was he doing here?

Seeing that she'd spotted him, Claude strode towards her, calling out, 'Good afternoon, Prudence. Lovely day for a spot of gardening.'

'Hello Claude. What brings you to Great Plumstead for the second time in a week?' Prue asked.

'Thought I'd come and check how you are. It's what Victor would have wanted me to do.'

'Really?' Prue had to stop herself from laughing out loud. 'Well, as you can see, I'm fine, getting on with things. In fact, you're lucky to have caught me. I'm due at Thea's shortly.' This wasn't true, but there was no way she was going to prolong Claude's visit and do as she normally would with visitors and invite him in for a cup of tea.

'Oh, right.' Claude looked a bit put out. 'I won't keep you then. Only I wondered when you were having Victor's will read?'

'We already have.'

'Shouldn't I have been informed?' he snapped.

Prue noticed a redness creeping up his neck to his face, betraying his feelings, just as it used to with Victor. It was clearly a family trait shared by the two brothers.

'No, not if you weren't needed there. Otherwise Mr Jefferson would have asked you to attend.' Prue walked towards the house.

'Wait!' Claude hurried after her. 'What about the business? Who did Victor leave it to?'

Prue halted and turned to face her brother-in-law, putting her hands on her hips. 'To his oldest son. To Jack. The same as your father left the business to Victor.'

'But, but...', Claude stammered, his face going puce. 'What about *me*? I should have at least had a share!'

'Not according to Victor. It was his choice who he left it to and you must accept that,' Prue said firmly.

'Then I'll contest the will and get what should rightly be mine!' Claude narrowed his icy blue eyes, reminding Prue so much of Victor that her breath caught in her throat.

Lifting her chin, she told him, 'The will is watertight. You'd be wasting your money to challenge it. I suggest you accept Victor's wishes and focus on your own business instead of sniffing around after other people's.'

Claude spluttered. 'How dare you talk to me like that?'

'I'll say what I please in my own home. Now I must go out so I'll bid you good day.' Leaving him standing there, Prue went inside, closing the kitchen door firmly behind her, her heart hammering in her chest as she turned the key. She'd been right thinking Claude would want his share, but he wouldn't get anything. She'd have to telephone Mr Jefferson in the morning to tell him of the visit, warn him in case Claude carried out his threat to contest the will.

She'd told Claude the truth but it was just as well he didn't know Jack intended to share the business with her and his siblings. Prue could imagine if he knew that, it would fuel Claude's desire for a part of the business for himself. She would keep that a closely guarded secret.

CHAPTER 34

'I still have to remind myself that you go along the *left*-hand side of the road in this country,' Lucille said as she pedalled her borrowed bicycle, riding beside Hettie. 'Just as well in London that I walk or travel by the underground or on buses.'

'It must be confusing,' Hettie acknowledged. 'I've never known any different.'

It was Sunday afternoon and the pair of them were out on a tour of Great Plumstead. Hettie had shown Lucille where she, Ada and their brothers had all gone to school, the church where they'd been christened and attended services and even the spot where Hettie's parents, who were Lucille's great-grandparents, were buried in the churchyard. Now they were heading for the cottage where Hettie had grown up and where her brothers had lived all their lives until they'd left for Canada.

Reaching a junction in the road, they braked and came to a halt as a convoy of military lorries rumbled past towards RAF Great Plumstead. The drivers put up their hands and waved to them as they drove by and Hettie and Lucille returned their waves with a smile.

'How far is the aerodrome from here?' Lucille asked.

'The main entrance gate is about a quarter of a mile that way.' Hettie pointed in the direction the lorries had gone. 'Your Aunt Ada's cottage was about half a mile that way too, just over the border into the next parish. Now it's demolished and what used to be her garden is concreted over to make a runway.'

'Poor Aunt Ada. She must have been so upset,' Lucille said as they set off again in the opposite direction to the lorries.

'She was, but as you'll see later, she's landed on her feet and is happy. The turning to the lane we want is just up beyond this bend. You can see the chimney pots of the cottage from here.' Hettie pointed to where they could be seen sticking up beside a small group of trees cloaked in fresh green leaves.

As they turned off the road onto a narrower lane, Hettie felt a stirring of homecoming. It might have been many years since she'd lived at Ivy Cottage, but it had been her first home and still held a special place in her heart, even if none of her family lived there anymore.

'How lovely, so cosy looking,' Lucille said as they came to a stop in front of the cottage which stood on its own, the nearest neighbour some fifty yards further down the lane.

'It was cosy all right but cramped with all of us living there. There are only two bedrooms. My parents had one and the other one had two beds in with a curtain hung between them. Ada and I shared a bed on one side of the curtain and Sidney and Albert the same on the other. Downstairs there's...' She paused as Hilda, the current tenant, came out of the front door and down the garden path to meet them.

'Hettie, I thought that was you,' Hilda greeted them with a smile. 'You out on WI business?'

'No, I'm on a trip down memory lane,' Hettie told the woman who was a fellow member of the village WI and seldom missed a meeting. 'This is my great-niece Lucille, who's here serving in the Canadian air force. She wanted to see where her grandpa, my brother Sidney, grew up.'

'Come on in and have a proper look around,' Hilda said, opening the garden gate. 'I remember Sidney – he was good pals with my brother Ted. They were older than me and in the top class at school when I was in the infants. I remember Sidney was always kind to us little ones.' She paused, beaming at Lucille. 'Fancy you coming here all these years later to see where he started out. Ted will be interested to hear you've visited. He moved in with me a few weeks ago. It's a shame he's out on Home Guard duties today as he'd have been pleased to meet his old pal's granddaughter.'

'Grandpa hoped I'd be able to visit where he grew up and I wanted to meet Aunt Hettie, so as soon as I got some leave I came,' Lucille explained as she leaned her bicycle beside Hettie's against the wall of the cottage. 'It's very different here to where I live in Canada. I'm loving getting to know it!'

'Come you on in then.' Hilda opened the door of the cottage and led them inside.

Back on their bicycles once more after a tour of Ivy Cottage and its garden, Hettie led the way towards their next stop at Great Plumstead Hall to see Ada.

'That must have brought back so many memories,' Lucille said, riding alongside Hettie.

'It certainly did. I could picture echoes and images of the past. Us all sitting around the table having our tea, one of my mother's beef and onion suet puddings. Playing cards with my brothers in front of the fire. Good times…' she sighed happily.

'How long has it been since you were last there?' Lucille asked.

'A long time. Must have been soon after my father died. I was living and working at the Hall then, Sidney and Albert were in Canada and Ada was married and had a home of her own. None of us wanted to carry on the tenancy, so after Dad died, a new tenant moved in,' Hettie explained. 'I enjoyed seeing the place again today. It was good of Hilda to show us around.'

'I think she liked it as much as we did,' Lucille said. 'She's a nice lady. I'll write about her in my letter to Grandpa. I'm sure going to have a lot to tell him.'

'There's plenty more to come yet,' Hettie said as they turned on to the long drive leading to the Hall. 'You're about to meet Ada, who'll love showing you around where she now lives.'

'Look at this place!' Lucille exclaimed as they emerged from the tree-lined drive on to the wide gravelled area in front of the large, honey-coloured hall. 'Aunt Ada lives here?'

Hettie laughed. 'Only in one wing and remember she's staff; she doesn't own the place. We need to head that way.' She pointed in the direction of the west wing where Ada was housekeeper.

'Even so, it's huge.' Lucille grinned at Hettie. 'I'm going to enjoy exploring.'

'Let's have a good look at you then.' Ada gave Lucille a shrewd once-over after she'd ushered them into her cosy housekeeper's sitting room in the west wing of the Hall. Then, after a small nod of satisfaction, Ada smiled warmly at the young woman. 'Fancy me having Sidney's granddaughter come and visit after all these years. You're very welcome, dear.'

Ada sat down on one of the armchairs in front of the fireplace. 'You sit there.' She gestured for Lucille to sit in the opposite chair. 'Hettie, would you mind fetching the tray of tea things from the kitchen for us, please? Everything's ready. You just need to add hot water to the teapot.' Without waiting for an answer, Ada turned to Lucille again. 'Now tell me all about yourself and what you're doing in London.'

Lucille glanced at Hettie, who gave her a reassuring wink. Nothing about the way Ada was behaving surprised Hettie. She'd known her older sister would take command and want to find out as much as she could about Sidney's granddaughter, and that was just to start with. After that Ada would move on to asking about Sidney, wanting to discover more than he'd ever told them in his letters over the years. Then there was their brother, Albert. Hettie chuckled to herself as she left the room and headed towards the kitchen. She was pleased for Ada. Her face as soon as she'd seen Lucille, the way it had lit up with joy and even a hint of tenderness, showed how much this visit meant to her sister. And to herself, too, Hettie thought. Having Lucille come to stay had brightened up their lives and Hettie hoped this wouldn't be their niece's only visit and that she'd return to see them again when she had more leave. They were Lucille's family and would be here for her while she was in England and so far from home.

CHAPTER 35

Thea was in a hurry this morning, pedalling hard towards the village, taking a delivery of freshly picked radishes, spring cabbage and broccoli to Barker's shop. This was one of her usual jobs, but on top of this and all the other tasks she'd planned to do today, she was going to have to fit in extra work in the garden. Nancy had telephoned at breakfast time to say that Marie had bad tummy ache and couldn't go to school, so she'd have to stay at home to look after her. Thea had been sympathetic as no one could help being ill and a poorly child would do better with their mother looking after them. Hopefully Marie would soon recover and return to school and Nancy could come back to work.

After arriving at Barker's in double quick time, Thea was unloading the baskets of vegetables from her bicycle when the shop door opened and Prue stepped out.

'Thea!' Prue greeted her happily.

'Hello, how are you?' Thea asked.

'Busy, you know.' Prue evaded the question. 'We start our deliveries for the Rural Pie Scheme today, so there's lots to sort out. I'm on the rota to deliver to the farms and we're also having a stall outside the village hall for anyone in the village who wants to buy something, seeing as we're a long way from a British Restaurant or canteen here.'

'That will keep you busy. How's Marie doing?'

Prue frowned. 'She's not herself and has become very clingy to Nancy which isn't like Marie at all. But if she's not feeling well then it's understandable. I remember whenever Edwin was ill when he was small, all he wanted was for me to hold him.'

'I hope Marie soon feels better.'

'Nancy at home looking after Marie makes you a worker short, but I'm sure she'll be better soon and back to school.' Prue glanced at her watch. 'I must get on or I'll be late picking up the pies.'

'Good luck today,' Thea called, watching her sister dash off in the direction of the bakers, thinking if there was anyone in this village who could make a success of the new Rural Pie Scheme it was Prue.

And yet, Thea's lingering thought was that she wished her sister would slow down and give herself more time to come to terms with what had recently happened to her. Though slowing down was hardly in Prue's nature, Thea knew that more than anyone.

CHAPTER 36

'I've got you down for a large cheese and onion pie,' Prue said, checking the list in her notebook.

'That's right,' her brother Reuben agreed.

He, like the other men working at Home Farm on the Great Plumstead Hall estate, had ordered and paid for their pies last week and now Prue was here delivering the freshly baked goods ready for their midday meal. She'd borrowed Gloria's pram to transport them; the baskets of pies fitted nicely where a baby would usually lie.

'I'll have another pie next time as well, a large meat and potato one.' While Prue wrote down Reuben's order for the following week, he checked the price list on display, then took his wallet from his jacket pocket and counted out the money into Prue's hand. 'There's a shilling and four pence.'

'Thank you. Help yourself to a large cheese and onion pie,' Prue instructed. 'I hope you enjoy it. They certainly smell good.'

'Makes a welcome change from sandwiches.' Reuben selected a pie and took a bite.' He chewed slowly, a look of pleasure blossoming on his face. After swallowing his mouthful, he gave Prue an appreciative nod. 'Delicious!'

'I'm glad to hear that. This scheme's an excellent idea and it looks like it's going down well.' She inclined her head towards where the other workers were sitting around in the sunshine, eating their own pies. 'Everyone's ordered another for next week so I'll be back with more then.'

'Where are you off to next?' Reuben asked.

'To the gardener's bothy by the Hall. The gardeners were keen to try the pies too,' Prue said. 'I'd better be going – there are more hungry workers waiting.'

Prue was on her way back towards the village, walking down the long tree-lined drive from Great Plumstead Hall, when she spotted a familiar figure emerging from the bluebell woods on the left with a dog trotting at her heels. It was Lady Campbell-Gryce.

The dog made to run towards Prue but was called back to heel by her Ladyship, who then raised her hand in greeting.

'Good afternoon, Prue,' Lady Campbell-Gryce said as she drew near. 'Whose baby have you got there?' She gestured towards the pram.

'There's no baby on board, only empty baskets. I've been delivering pies for the new Rural Pie Scheme and just made my last delivery to your gardeners.'

'I hope they appreciated your efforts,' her Ladyship said.

'They did and were tucking in as I left. Today's our first day and the deliveries have gone down well. We've also got a stall set up in the village, for people to collect their pies from,' Prue told her.

'You do an enormous amount for this village and are to be

much admired for your effort and hard work.' Lady Campbell-Gryce paused for a moment, stroking the ears of her dog, who sat leaning against her legs. 'How are you feeling? Are you bearing up after your recent loss?' Her voice was kind and her eyes sympathetic.

'I'm fine.' Prue wondered how many times she'd uttered that vague phrase in the past twelve days since Victor had been killed. 'Being busy helps,' she added, keeping her voice light.

'It's still an enormous shock to lose your husband and in such tragic circumstances.'

'But he was with his mistress!' The words came blurting out before Prue had a chance to stop them. She gasped, slapping a hand over her mouth as if to retract the revelation, but it was too late. The secret was out. The truth revealed.

Lady Campbell-Gryce's eyes widened and she took a few moments before she replied, 'Oh my dear, I'm so terribly sorry. That's even worse... I understand, I really do.'

The kind words brought tears to Prue's eyes and she couldn't stop them spilling over and running down her cheeks. She fumbled to get a handkerchief from her handbag, but before she could find one, Lady Campbell-Gryce pressed a clean, ironed white handkerchief into Prue's hand.

'Here, take this.'

'Thank you.' Prue dabbed at her face with the soft cloth and took some steadying breaths to get a hold on her emotions. This sort of behaviour wasn't her way, especially not in public — and particularly not in front of her Ladyship.

'Did you know what was going on?'

Prue nodded. 'Yes, I have for a while. Victor's Sunday meetings every week in Norwich were false. He went there to see her. I didn't mind that much because our marriage was... well, it wasn't a happy one. I thought she was welcome to him, to be honest.' As she spoke Prue realised it felt good to talk to someone about this. 'He went to Norwich that night to be with her because she was scared after the first heavy raid. He was with her at her house when it got bombed. Thea and I went there after our shift in the WVS canteen and saw them both brought out. She was injured, and he was dead.'

'Oh, my goodness!' Lady Campbell-Gryce exclaimed. 'How dreadful for you to see that! I'm so sorry.' She put her hand on Prue's arm. 'That really is so terribly hard for you.'

Prue nodded. 'It was, but we haven't made it common knowledge. Only my sisters and Hettie know the truth. I don't want my children to find out, or to have how Victor behaved taint our family and make us a target for village gossips.'

'I promise I will never breathe a word of it to anyone.' Her Ladyship took a deep breath. 'In fact, I understand very well what it's like for your husband to have a mistress. My husband has one and she's not the first. Knowing him, she won't be the last either.'

Prue was shocked at this revelation. 'I'm sorry to hear that.'

Lady Campbell-Gryce pressed her lips into a thin line and let out a sigh. 'It is not uncommon when you scratch beneath the surface, especially among people like me. Our marriages are more about family expectations and making what's perceived as a *good match* to keep connections, land and money. It's rarely about marrying for love and I certainly didn't love Anthony when I married him. I've *never* loved him! When he took a mistress not long after we married, I wasn't surprised and was rather glad. So you see I do understand and trust you to keep my secret too. I know how much keeping busy helps give one a purpose and I enjoy working at the hospital so much. It's made such a difference to me.'

'You'd never know all that was going on for you,' Prue said. 'Same as for me, I suppose. Appearances can be deceptive. I never loved Victor either. I married him because I wanted to be a mother and he had two small boys who needed one after their own mother died. With so many men lost in the Great War, it seemed like my only chance.'

'What a pair we are, and you'd never suspect it about either of us from outward appearances.' Lady Campbell-Gryce gave a soft laugh. 'How about coming back with me for a spot of lunch and you can tell me more about this Rural Pie Scheme and all the other things you do to keep busy? I'd love to know more. And perhaps I could help with some things too. I've heard excellent reports about your Mother's Day Club and what fun is had there, as well as the good work it does for the community.'

'Thank you, that would be lovely,' Prue said, glad to accept the offer. They might be from different classes, but they had a shared experience. Having someone to talk to who truly understood was a relief and if Lady Campbell-Gryce really was interested in getting involved with The Mother's Day Club then she'd be more than welcome.

CHAPTER 37

The sound of loud knocking on her bedroom door woke Thea with a start. She'd been in a deep sleep and the sudden launch into wakefulness left her feeling disorientated for a few moments.

The door opened and Hettie stepped inside, the light from a candle lighting up her face. 'The air-raid siren's going off in Wykeham. We need to get to the shelter.'

'I was sound asleep,' Thea paused, cocking her head to one side, and she could just make out the faint wail of the siren coming across the four miles from Wykeham. 'Thanks Hettie.' She threw back her covers and got up, pulled on her dressing gown and pushed her feet into her slippers. 'Where are the children?'

'Flo and Evie are taking them out to the shelter. You're the last one to wake up and no wonder after the hours you've put into the garden this week. Just get yourself downstairs as quick as you can. You've been working too hard and it's taking its toll on you.' Hettie gave Thea a concerned look before turning and heading off to the shelter.

Thea couldn't argue with her friend's parting comment. It was true. She'd put in a lot of extra hours working out in Rookery House's gardens this week, even going back out to work again after tea and not stopping until the darkness forced her inside. But if she hadn't, then they'd get behind with the many tasks that needed doing. Crops wouldn't be looked after properly and the yields would be down. With Nancy off work caring for Marie, who was still unwell, Thea had been forced to fill in. Thea had known taking on Nancy was a risk, both for her lack of experience and for having children to care for. And now that they were halfway through Nancy's three-month trial period, her time off work was becoming a real concern.

Hurrying down the stairs and outside, Thea caught up with the others as they were going into the Anderson. Marianne had settled a drowsy Emily on the little bed that crossed the back of the shelter, and was cradling a still sleeping baby Bea against her chest as she took a seat on one of the benches running along the length of the Anderson. Flo and Evie organised George and Betty to sit next to them, wrapping the children in blankets to keep warm, while Hettie stowed the basket with flasks of hot drink under the other bench and then sat down.

Glancing up at the dark sky where the stars were blotted out by thick cloud, Thea couldn't see or even hear any planes yet. But that didn't mean there wouldn't be any and it was always best to head to the shelter when the air-raid warning sounded, even if the skies were clear. Closing the door behind her, she sat next to Hettie.

'Put this over you to keep warm.' Hettie handed Thea a blanket. 'It might be mid-May but it's still cool at night and who knows how long we'll be in here.'

'Not long, I hope,' Evie said. 'My shifts are always harder

after time spent in here. I don't want Matron Reed breathing down my neck because I've made a mistake through tiredness.'

'I can understand that!' Thea gave the young woman a sympathetic smile. 'Whenever I've been to the hospital on WVS duties and encountered Matron, she's always made me feel like I've done something wrong, and I don't even work there!'

'She has that effect on people,' Evie agreed.

As tiredness stole over them, their conversation dried up. George and Betty fell asleep, each of them snuggling up against the young woman they sat next to. Thea could feel herself drifting off, her head falling down and waking her up with a jolt a few times before she leaned it back against the wall of the shelter and let sleep claim her.

Thea had no idea how long she'd been asleep when the sound of a plane's engines broke into her dreams, starting her into wakefulness. Snapping her heavy-lidded eyes open, she looked around her and saw that everyone else was awake, except for the children who slept on oblivious.

'One of theirs,' Hettie mouthed, pointing upwards, having recognised the vroom-vroom beat of the enemy plane's unsynchronised engines which were so different from the smoother rhythm of the RAF's planes.

Thea willed it to pass over as fast as possible. She could feel the tension building in the confined space of the Anderson as they listened to the engines growing louder until the plane was right above them. It went over and gradually the noise faded as it flew off into the distance until the night-time sounds of the countryside were all they could hear.

Hettie let out a soft sigh, shaking her head. 'It always puts the wind up me hearing them,' she said in a hushed voice. 'Makes my heart race.' She placed a hand on her chest.

Thea grabbed hold of the older woman's free hand and squeezed it. 'Thankfully it was only the one. Probably got lost and just passing over on its way back home.'

'Let's hope so,' Hettie agreed.

After that, Thea found it impossible to fall asleep again. Her mind wouldn't be still and the shelter wasn't the most comfortable place either. When the all-clear sounded across the miles from Wykeham half an hour later, she was enormously grateful to traipse back to bed, where she hoped that sleep would soon come. Tomorrow was going to be another busy day in the garden and she needed as much energy as she could muster.

CHAPTER 38

It was Saturday morning, and Thea was planting out some of the young tomato plants they'd grown from seed into a vegetable bed, where they'd mature, flower and bare fruit. She loved the sharp smell of the plants; it reminded her of summer days picking glossy red — and very delicious — sun-ripened tomatoes. But the prospect of doing that was some weeks off yet, Thea reminded herself. In the meantime, planting out was a satisfying task and if this year's crop of tomatoes was anything like last year's, there would be a bumper harvest.

So much about her work involved being patient. You couldn't rush things but had to wait for the plants to grow and accept that variables like the weather were a huge uncontrollable factor in the process too.

It was so different from her previous job running her business in London, but Thea loved her new role. Working outside on a beautiful, warm and sunshine-filled May morning like this was a delight, even if she did feel so tired. With the number of jobs that she had to get through today, she could have done without an air raid disturbing her sleep last night. After they'd returned to the house, she'd managed about three hours, but it hadn't felt like anywhere near enough when her alarm clock had startled her awake again a little after six this morning.

Normally on a Saturday Thea would work in the morning and then have the afternoon off to spend with George and Betty, but today she was going to have to keep working all day. With Nancy having missed a whole week's work, there were a lot of jobs to catch up on. Flo had volunteered to do more, but Thea didn't expect her to do too much extra as the young woman needed her rest and time to do other things she enjoyed, like her singing group in the village. Running Rookery House's gardens was Thea's responsibility. It lay on her shoulders and no one else's.

She'd just finished digging a hole with a trowel for the next tomato plant to go in, when she heard her name being shouted. Turning around, she saw Betty running towards her.

'Auntie Thea, come and look at what we've found!' Betty called, beckoning to her. 'Come and see! George is watching over it.'

'What is it?' Thea got to her feet, brushing soil off her hands.

'I don't know but it wasn't there before and it's made a hole in the grass,' Betty said.

A sense of unease crept through Thea as she took hold of Betty's hand. What could it be? she wondered as they hurried through Five Acres field towards the meadow area where the grass was growing longer, ready to be cut and dried for their hay crop sometime in June. George stood waiting about a quarter of the way in. As they approached, he held up something in the air, calling out, 'Look what we found!'

Thea's stomach clenched as she stared at the flat piece of metal that George held out to her. Taking the cold metal from him, she studied it closely, thinking it looked like a fin, the sort she'd seen attached to the end of bombs in diagrams in the newspaper. It was slightly bent where it had sheared off. One thing was certain, it hadn't been here before and wasn't something that had been turned up in ploughing the way old animal bones sometimes were. This was new.

'Where did you find this?' she asked.

'Just here.' George pointed to where there was a gash in the ground, the exposed brown soil contrasting sharply with the surrounding green grass.

Thea could see no sign of the bomb on the surface, just an indent in the crumbly soil a couple of feet wide and about three long, which gave off the scent of freshly turned earth. It must be deeper down, the force of its impact driving it into the ground. The enemy plane that flew over last night while they were in the Anderson shelter could have dropped it. Now it lay, a literal ticking bomb under their feet which could blow up at any moment, Thea thought, her heart pounding. They needed to get away from it as quickly as possible, but carefully, so they didn't trigger it to explode.

'What do you think it is?' Betty asked, pointing at the fin.

'I'm not sure. It might be an old bit of metal from something,' Thea said vaguely. 'Let's take it back to the house and show Hettie.' She fought to keep her voice calm, not wanting to alarm the children. 'We'll play fairy footsteps and tread as lightly as we can.'

Betty gave her a funny look, probably wondering why Auntie Thea should suddenly want to play fairy footsteps, but she didn't argue. With her blood thrumming in her ears, Thea led the children slowly and gently away from the unexploded bomb, each of them treading softly and lightly.

'That's it, keep going,' Thea encouraged them, all the while fighting the urge to shout *run*, but fearing any heavier vibrations from their footsteps might be enough to detonate the bomb.

As soon as they'd passed through the gate and were a good hundred yards from the bomb, she changed tack, wanting to get them as far from it as quickly as possible. 'Fairy footsteps are over. Who's going to be first back to the house, with fast, giant's footsteps? On your marks, get set, go!'

She watched with relief as the pair of them rushed off ahead of her to the house, each wanting to be the first to reach it. Hurrying on behind, the thought of what could have happened seemed to run through her, wrapping around her heart like an icy grip. How George had stood there waiting by an unexploded bomb while his sister went to fetch her. Thea shuddered. Thankfully nothing bad had occurred yet and she shouldn't waste precious energy thinking about what could have when she must concentrate on what needed to be done now. Of one thing she was certain – until this bomb was dealt with, the children had to be elsewhere for their safety. She'd see if they could go to Prue's.

'What did George and Betty find in the grass in Five Acres?' Hettie asked as Thea went into the kitchen.

'This.' Thea held up the metal fin.

Hettie stared at it. 'What is that?'

'Where are the children?' Thea asked, surprised that they weren't in the kitchen.

'Washing their hands in the scullery. I was going to give them a drink of milk and then noticed the state of their hands, all covered in soil. So I sent them to clean them first.' Hettie gave Thea a searching look. 'What's the matter? What is that thing you've got there?' She pointed at the piece of metal, her eyes curious behind her round glasses.

Thea glanced over at the door to the scullery, which was slightly ajar and through which she could hear the children talking.

'I think it's a tail fin from a bomb!' she whispered, seeing the colour drain from Hettie's face. 'Which means there's an unexploded bomb embedded in the ground in our hay meadow. The children found this on the surface and the rest of the bomb's ploughed down into the earth, so there's nothing to see but a gash in the soil. We need to call for the bomb disposal squad and get all the children out of here until it's made safe.'

'They could have been...' Hettie's words tailed off as she put a hand over her mouth.

Thea nodded. 'I know. I haven't told them what it is – I don't want to scare them. I'm going to see if Prue will look after them at her house. Marianne must take Emily and Bea there too. Can you get them organised and ready to leave as quick as you can while I make some phone calls?'

'Of course.' Hettie gave Thea's arm a squeeze. 'You do what you need to. We'll get the children to safety right away.'

'We'll be guarding the UXB in three-hour shifts around the clock until the bomb disposal squad arrives,' Reuben, who was a sergeant in the village Home Guard, informed Thea as they stood in the garden near the back of the house. He'd hurried home from work after being contacted by the police and having quickly changed into his khaki uniform, he had been ready and waiting when three other members of the Home Guard arrived at Rookery House to assist him.

'How long until the bomb squad get here?' Thea asked.

'I don't know. They'll be here as soon as they can. It

depends on what other jobs they've got,' Reuben said. 'Every unexploded bomb is given a category depending on the most urgent need. Bombs in cities where there's danger to more people, buildings and things like gas and water pipes get priority. This bomb's in the middle of a hay field so it's less urgent. How long it will be all depends on what other higher priority UXBs there are that need defusing first.'

'But it could explode at any time!' Thea said.

'I know and that's why no one must go near it. You need to keep in the house for your own safety. At least it's far enough from the bomb that you don't have to be evacuated.'

'What about Primrose?' Thea asked, thinking of the gentle cow who was grazing in the field adjoining Five Acres. An explosion would terrify the poor animal and it could be even worse if she were hit by the blast or shrapnel fragments from it.

'I'll bring her into the byre. She'll be safer in there and can eat hay all day. She might not like being inside but it won't hurt her. Better than...' Reuben put his hand on Thea's shoulder. 'I'll shut the piglets and rabbits inside as well. Now go indoors and *stay* there.' His blue eyes met Thea's and she nodded.

'I will, don't worry. It's just me, Hettie and Flo here now. I promise we'll stay inside until you tell us we can come out.' Thea was relieved that Prue had been willing to shelter the children at her house and Marianne had taken them there. They'd all remain at Prue's until it was safe to return home again.

Reuben turned his attention to the members of the Home Guard, ordering one to patrol the gateway into Rookery House's drive from the road and watch out for the bomb disposal squad's arrival. Then he led the two other men towards Five Acres field.

Turning to go indoors, Thea spotted two faces at the taped kitchen window – Hettie and Flo had been watching what was going on. This wasn't how any of them had planned on spending today, but with a UXB buried in the earth not far away, their plans had flown out of the window, Thea thought as she made her way indoors to tell the others what was happening.

'So we don't know how long we're going to be stuck in here or when the bomb squad will arrive?' Hettie asked.

'No.' Thea sat down at the kitchen table. 'There'll be members of the Home Guard here making sure no one approaches the bomb and all we can do is wait and hope it doesn't blow up before the bomb squad defuses it.'

'Well, there's one thing I *can* be doing while we're waiting,' Hettie said, bustling across the kitchen and reaching for her wrap-around pinafore which hung from a hook on the pantry door. 'And that's bake. Those men out there will need feeding, and so will the bomb squad. We can prepare for that. Make some currant buns, Norfolk shortcakes and plenty of bread rolls for filling with some of the cream cheese I made yesterday. The cheese will go nicely with pickled beetroot in a fresh bread roll.'

Thea looked at Flo, who stood by the sink. 'Shall we help bake since we can't do anything in the garden today?'

Flo nodded. 'I'm willing. It will make a nice change and I haven't baked anything for ages.'

'You've just got yourself two willing assistants then, Hettie,' Thea said with a smile.

~

It was nearly three o'clock when Flo came flying into the kitchen from the sitting room where she'd been on lookout. 'They're here!'

Thea heaved a sigh of relief, putting the plate she'd just washed up onto the wooden drying rack at the side of the sink. The past four hours had seemed far longer than usual while they'd waited for the bomb squad to arrive. They'd invited the first shift of Home Guard in for something to eat after they had finished their three-hour watch and been replaced by the second shift. The men had gratefully tucked into some of the results of their baking session and had not long gone home.

Thea had kept herself busy while they'd been shut inside but was all the while aware of the bomb lying buried in Five Acres hay meadow waiting to explode at any moment. It felt like an ominous presence lurking beneath the ground. Now Thea hoped it would be safely defused and removed, so they could get back to normal without the threat of a sudden explosion hanging over them.

'Let's go and see.' Hettie hurried out of the kitchen and through to the sitting room.

Thea followed and, along with Flo, the three of them peered out of the bay window at the goings-on. A lorry was now parked in front of the house and men were jumping out of the back. An officer and sergeant were talking to the member of the Home Guard who'd been on sentry duty at the gate and who was pointing in the direction of Five Acres field.

Spotting them at the window, the officer touched the brim of his cap and then his attention turned to Reuben, who must have heard their arrival and come to meet them.

'What are they saying?' Hettie said, straining to hear as the men talked.

'I can't make it out,' Thea said. 'But I suppose Reuben's

briefing him on the situation.' She was worried about her brother who, apart from a brief visit to the house for a drink and something to eat when the Home Guard shifts changed over, had remained outside watching over things. He wasn't limiting his duty to three-hour shifts, but then as a sergeant he had more responsibility, and the bomb was not far from where he lived either.

Leaving most of the men waiting near the lorry, Reuben, the officer and his sergeant disappeared in the direction of Five Acres field and the bomb.

'It's no good. I need to know what's going on!' Hettie heaved up the sash window and beckoned to the soldiers with her hand.

A corporal came over and crouched down near the open sash window so he could speak through it. 'Are you all right in there?' he asked.

'We want to know what's going on,' Hettie said.

'They've gone to have a look at the UXB – see what needs doing. They'll probe down with a rod to see how deep the bomb is and then it will be our job to dig down to it so the Lieutenant can defuse it,' he explained.

'Are you hungry?' Hettie asked. 'We've been baking while we waited so we can keep you well fed. We've made Norfolk shortcakes, currant buns...'

'That sounds delicious,' the corporal smiled. 'And yes, we'd love some of your baking later, if that's all right. Once we've done our job and the bomb's made safe.'

'How long do you think it will take?' Thea asked.

'It depends on how deep the bomb is.' The corporal lifted a shoulder. 'I'd better get the men organised and ready. Keep yourselves safely indoors, won't you?'

He stood up and joined the rest of the soldiers who were now unloading equipment from the back of the truck –

wheelbarrows, shovels, planks of woods, saws, sandbags and other paraphernalia they'd need to do their job.

It must have only been a matter of five to ten minutes before the officer and sergeant returned and ordered the unit into action. Pushing wheelbarrows piled with equipment and carrying shovels over their shoulders, the men headed back around the side of the house towards where the bomb had fallen.

'Now all we can do is wait again.' Hettie let out a heavy sigh. 'I'm going to do some knitting to occupy my fingers.' She went off to the kitchen.

'She's worried,' Flo said after Hettie had left the room.

'I know, we all are. This isn't exactly what we expected to happen today.' Thea closed the window. 'What are you going to do while we wait?'

'I think I'll write a letter to my grandparents,' Flo said. 'I'll be up in my bedroom if you need me.'

Left alone in the sitting room, Thea thought of the many jobs she should have been doing in the garden today, all of which were even more behind schedule now. She decided to go up to her bedroom and have a nap to try to make up for missed sleep from last night, because as soon as the bomb was defused, she needed to get back outside and working again — and carry on for as long as there was light enough to see by.

When Thea came downstairs a couple of hours later, she found that Hettie had company in the kitchen – two of the members of the Home Guard who were on duty from the second shift. One was Alf Barker from the grocer's shop and the other a man she didn't recognise.

'Hello,' Thea said, giving them a welcoming smile. 'What's happening out there? Have they defused it yet?'

'They've finished the digging and the men have retreated behind the safety point they set up. Now it's the officer's turn to do his bit,' Alf told her. 'We've been sent in here out of the way and to get some of Hettie's baking to take out to the men as soon as the bomb's made safe. They've been looking forward to it.'

'How will you know when it's safe?' Thea asked.

'They'll blow a whistle. Unless, of course, there's an explosion first.' Alf grimaced.

'Let's hope that's not the case,' Hettie said with a shudder of her shoulders. 'Thea, I don't think you've met Ted before, have you?' She gestured towards the other man, who'd stood quietly listening. 'Ted, this is my very good friend Thea Thornton and Thea, this is Ted Ellison.'

'Pleased to meet you.' Ted stepped forwards and held out his hand to Thea. 'I knew your parents, and you too, when you were small. I grew up here in Great Plumstead but moved away for work many years ago. I've recently come back and joined the village Home Guard platoon.'

Thea shook his hand. She liked the look of him, with his silvery hair and kind hazel eyes, and he had a gentle way about him. 'What work took you away?'

'Gardening. I ended up as head gardener at a hall in Suffolk before I retired. I've moved back to live with my sister,' Ted said.

'That's Hilda who lives in Ivy Cottage where I grew up,' Hettie said. 'Remember, I took Lucille there when she was visiting. Ted was a friend of my brother Sidney. They were the same age.'

Thea opened her mouth to speak, but the piercing shrill

note of a whistle being blown outside made her pause. 'Is that the all-clear signal? That the bomb's been defused?'

'Sounds like it,' Alf said. 'I'll check.' He hurried outside and returned moments later with one of the soldiers who, from the way he was breathing fast, must have run over from the safety point to inform them.

'All's well!' Alf announced coming into the kitchen with a look of satisfaction on his face.

'It was a 250kg bomb, but it's been defused now and is safe,' the soldier told them. 'We'll take it away with us and blow it up on the marshes. But first, the corporal has sent me to help bring out some of your baking for the men if the offer's still there.' He grinned cheekily, looking hopeful.

'Of course it is. It won't take me long to get it ready.' Hettie fetched two baskets from the pantry and began to pack one with the plates of baking, each covered in clean tea towels, that were standing ready on the table.

'Can I help?' Ted asked.

'You fill this up,' Hettie said, handing him the other basket. 'Thank you.'

'The air-raid siren went off last night and we heard one enemy plane flying right overhead,' Thea said. 'Do you think it dropped the bomb? There haven't been any others over recently and the bomb definitely wasn't there before today.'

The soldier nodded. 'It probably jettisoned it on its way back from wherever it had been. We find quite a few of them in the middle of the countryside and not gone off. Lucky this one landed in the field rather than on the house.'

'And luckily it didn't explode,' Thea said solemnly.

'Right, these are ready,' Hettie interrupted, handing a basket to the soldier, while Ted carried the other. 'I hope you all enjoy them and please pass on our heartfelt thanks to all the men. Ted, you and Alf enjoy them too,' Hettie added. 'You've done your bit this afternoon.'

After the men had gone, Thea and Hettie stood by the kitchen window looking out at the garden.

'Thank goodness that's over,' Hettie said. 'I've never been so grateful for the soothing process of baking in all my life as I have today.'

Thea put her arm around her friend's shoulders. 'Those men will appreciate your efforts making them delicious food. It must be hard doing the job they do day after day. It's such dangerous work.'

Hettie nodded. 'I know it's wartime but I never thought we'd come that close to a bomb here at Rookery House.'

'We must count our blessings that it landed where it did,' Thea said. 'And it's why we should never get complacent in an air raid and stay in bed instead of going out to the shelter. I know it's a nuisance and loses us sleep, but better that than if Rookery House ever got hit!'

CHAPTER 39

Prue straightened up, rubbing her hands on her lower back, and looked with satisfaction at the small, fresh green lettuce plants she'd just planted out at the WI allotment.

'It won't be long before they're ready to pick and sell on our WI stall on market day,' Gloria called across from where she was crouched down, planting out a similar row of lettuces.

'We'll need to plant some more in a fortnight to keep the supply going.' Prue got to her feet and stretched her arms above her head to relieve her muscles after bending over. She enjoyed the physical work here but was always careful to be mindful and not pull a muscle because she had too many other things to do to find herself hampered by a bad back.

Prue and Gloria were spending Sunday afternoon at the allotment, making the most of the fine day. Gloria's little girl Dora was being looked after by her landlady, Sylvia.

After planting her last lettuce, Gloria stood up and, following Prue's lead, stretched. She was dressed in a pair of dungarees rather than in one of her usual close-fitting, brightly coloured dresses, although her dungarees were much brighter than the drab brown ones worn by the local Land Girls, Gloria having made hers from some red floral curtains.

'What have you got planned for this coming week apart from Mother's Day Club?' Gloria asked.

'I'm out in the WVS canteen and delivering food for the Pie Scheme,' Prue said. 'And there's another job I need to do at home, but I keep putting it off. I really must get it done.'

'What's that? It sounds ominous and not like you to put off a task that needs doing.' Gloria arched one of her shaped eyebrows, giving Prue an enquiring look.

Prue glanced across the allotments to where she could see Percy Blake busy at work hoeing on his plot. Letting out a sigh, she returned her gaze to her friend and said, 'I need to sort out Victor's things. I've decided to donate his clothes to the WVS in Norwich for those who lost their homes in the bombing. Then there's his study to go through, papers to check and so on.'

'I'd be glad to 'elp,' Gloria said. 'It ain't an easy job sorting through things after someone dies. I remember my old mum couldn't face doing it after my dad died. It was a year or more before she could bring herself to do it and she wouldn't let anyone else do it for her, either. I think while they were in the 'ouse it made her feel like part of 'im was still there.'

Prue didn't feel that way about Victor's things. Quite the opposite. She was keen to get rid of them but was putting off the task because seeing them, touching them, would remind her of Victor. Bring back unpleasant memories of him. However, she couldn't put it off for ever and perhaps tackling it sooner rather than later would be better, plus it would free up valuable space in the house.

'All right, thank you. I'd like to accept your kind offer.' Prue gave Gloria an appreciative smile. Doing the job with her cheerful friend would make it so much easier.

'Excellent. I ain't got nothing planned on Tuesday afternoon and I'm sure Sylvia would happily mind Dora for me for a couple of hours again. Are you free then?'

Prue thought for a moment, mentally ticking off her commitments for the week. 'Yes, I could do that. Tuesday afternoon it is.'

CHAPTER 40

Thea removed Primrose's halter and stroked under the gentle cow's chin, enjoying a few moments of calm on this beautiful May morning. Spring had cloaked the countryside in shades of green and with a forget-me-not-blue sky overhead, the world felt fresh and clean with no UXBs lurking under the hay meadow to worry about.

'Off you go and enjoy the new grass.' Thea patted Primrose's shoulder, then walked to the gate out of the field. After closing it behind her, Thea folded her arms and leaned them on the top bar, taking a moment to watch Primrose grazing and think through the day ahead.

It was Monday morning, the start of a new week, and there was plenty to do. After last week's long days of work, Nancy's return today would be a relief. Having a third pair of hands to do the jobs would take the pressure off Thea and get them back on track with the many necessary tasks that had to be done to keep the gardens at Rookery House running smoothly.

With a last glance at Primrose, Thea headed to the house.

She'd already taken the pail of milk in after she'd finished milking and now, with all the animals fed and let out, it was time for her breakfast. Flo had seen to the chickens, pigs and rabbits and should be back indoors by now to have hers.

After washing her hands thoroughly at the scullery sink, Thea went into the kitchen to join everyone else. Marianne and Flo were serving up helpings of porridge and stewed plums for the children and Hettie was pouring out cups of tea. It looked a happy family scene, Thea thought, her stomach rumbling with hunger. But one look from Hettie made Thea stop. Something was wrong. She raised a questioning eyebrow at the older woman, who gave a nod in the direction Thea had just come from. Getting the message, Thea returned to the scullery and was soon joined by Hettie, who closed the kitchen door behind her.

'What's the matter?' Thea asked.

'Nancy telephoned. Marie's still poorly so she's going to take her to the doctor this morning,' Hettie informed her. 'It must be something serious and I hope the doctor can help the little girl. But I'm afraid it means you're a worker short again. I hoped Nancy would be back today after being off all last week.'

'So did I,' Thea admitted. 'But if Marie's ill, then she's ill. She can't help it. This was what worried me about taking on someone with other responsibilities. It's not the same as with Flo.'

'It's a trial job, though,' Hettie reminded her. 'Maybe it's just not going to work out. Nancy was very apologetic and said she hates letting you down.'

'I know, and she's very keen and conscientious about her work when she is here. I can't fault her on that. But I do need her here to do the work.'

'Let me help. I can sow some seeds or something,' Hettie said.

'Thank you. I appreciate that and there are some seeds you can plant today if you're willing and have the time. We're pushed keeping up with everything with how fast things are growing, especially the weeds.'

'I'm on shift at The Mother's Day Club this morning, but I can help you this afternoon when I get back.' Hettie gave Thea's arm a pat. 'Now come and have some breakfast. You need to keep your strength up.'

'I'll be right there.' Thea watched her friend return to the kitchen then took a moment before she joined the others; she had to rethink the plan for today. Which tasks needed to be prioritised and which ones could wait. She let out a heavy sigh. It looked like being another very long and busy day again.

CHAPTER 41

'If we put this here...' Marianne placed a brown-paper pattern piece on the tweedy material, 'it avoids that thin, worn-out patch but still follows the grain.'

'This fabric will make a lovely child's coat when it's done,' Hettie said, carefully pinning the pattern to secure it in place.

She and Marianne were at The Mother's Day Club in the village hall, where the members were spending the morning working on garments for the clothing depot. By making do and mending, or the careful repurposing of still useable sections of material from worn-out clothes, they were able to make new things from old.

As usual, there was a children's corner where some women were looking after all the youngsters, leaving their mothers free to do the work.

'If you get all the pieces cut out then I'll start sewing it together,' Marianne said. 'Providing Emily and Bea don't need me.' She glanced over to where her older daughter was playing a game with Gloria's little girl Dora, involving the tea set, which they loved more than any of the other toys. Baby Bea was having a nap in her pram, which was parked nearby and under the watch of the mothers caring for the children.

'Marianne, can you come and 'ave a look at this for me?' Gloria called over from the table where she was working on a pair of trousers. 'I think I've gone wrong somewhere.'

'I'll be right there,' Marianne said. 'Let me know when you've finished cutting out, Hettie.'

'Will do.'

Hettie always felt more comfortable with knitting needles in her hands than a sewing needle or anything involved with dressmaking. But with the need to keep up the supply of garments for the clothing depot, she was willing to challenge herself to help as much as she could. At least she had Marianne's expert guidance to assist her.

Now with all the pattern pieces securely pinned on the unpicked material from what had been a man's coat, all Hettie had to do was cut them out. Although that wasn't as simple as it sounded. She needed to concentrate so that she didn't make a hole where she shouldn't and ruin the fabric. There's no rush, Hettie told herself. Look first, check again and only cut when you're quite sure. She picked up the heavy dressmaking scissors and got to work.

Hettie finished cutting out the last piece, placed it on the pile of other already cut-out bits and, with a satisfied sigh, put the dressmaking scissors down on the table.

'You made that look so easy,' a familiar plummy voice said.

Turning around, Hettie was surprised to see Lady Campbell-Gryce sitting on a chair nearby. Hettie had been so engrossed in her work she hadn't been aware that she was being watched.

'Your Ladyship, I didn't know you were there.' Hettie gave her former employer a welcoming smile.

'I've only been here for a moment. I didn't want to disturb you because you looked so absorbed in what you were doing. It's fascinating to watch you and all the others. You're all so productive.' Lady Campbell-Gryce gestured towards the other women busy at work on the tables set out around the hall. Some were sewing with machines, others hand stitching or unpicking an old garment.

It wasn't any wonder no one had noticed they had a visitor, Hettie thought. Everyone was so focused on what they were doing.

'We're making garments for our clothing depot,' Hettie said. 'With the children growing so quickly and more people needing help in the village, our stock soon gets depleted.'

'Yes, I've heard about that. Prue told me about the work you do, and that's why I'm here. Your sister Mrs Kilburn has been helping me to sort through various items that have been stored in the attics and which might be useful here. Blankets, curtains and old clothes, that type of thing. There are far more things than I could ever need. I wondered if I could donate them to be used for the clothing depot?'

'I should think so. Prue's the one to ask though, not me.' Hettie scanned around the hall looking for her friend but couldn't see her. 'She must be in the kitchen preparing for the tea break. I'll go and get her.'

'Thank you. While you're doing that, I shall bring some samples in from the car for Prue to see.'

While Lady Campbell-Gryce went outside, Hettie hurried into the village hall kitchen, where she found Prue setting out cups on the trolley.

'You're never going to believe who's just arrived,' Hettie said.

'Who?' Prue asked.

'Lady Campbell-Gryce! She's brought some old curtains and things to use for the clothing depot.'

Prue stared incredulously at Hettie for a moment, her face slowly breaking into a smile. 'That is a nice surprise. I was telling her about it last week. She was very interested in what we do here, but she never said anything about donating material. If she's offering, then we won't say no!'

'You'd best come and have a look,' Hettie encouraged her.

Prue followed Hettie out into the hall and to the outside door where they met her Ladyship coming in with a pile of what looked like curtains and blankets in her arms.

'Let me take them for you?' Prue offered.

'No, it's fine, I can manage thank you,' Lady Campbell-Gryce said. 'I'll put them down here and you can take a proper look to see if you think they're suitable.' She placed the armful on the chair she'd been sitting on earlier, took a dark blue velvet curtain off the top and held it up so the material pooled down to the floor.

'There's a lot of fabric there, yards of it.' Prue stepped forwards and felt the soft cloth between her finger and thumb. 'Are you sure about wanting to donate this? It's good quality material!'

'Absolutely, it's just been lying inside chests in the attics. Far better to use it.'

By now, the other women of The Mother's Day Club had realised something was going on and had stopped what they were doing to watch.

'Marianne, what do *you* think?' Lady Campbell-Gryce called over to where she'd been helping Edith with her sewing. 'Do come and give your expert opinion.'

Marianne made her way across the hall and felt the cloth

just as Prue had done. 'It's lovely fabric and would be ideal for winter dresses or jackets.'

'They would be useful additions to your clothing depot, wouldn't they, Prue?' her Ladyship asked. 'And how about this?' She pointed at the folded table cloth on top of the pile. 'What could you make from it?'.

'That would make a lovely dress or some blouses,' Marianne said, running her hand over the smooth, brightly patterned cloth.

'Excellent!' Lady Campbell-Gryce gave a winning smile. 'Please say yes, Prue. I have a car full of fabric and want to donate the lot. I dread to think of the look on Mrs Kilburn's face if I have to take it home again and ask her to repack it in the attic. She would not be happy.'

'I can imagine that very well,' Hettie said with a grin.

'I think we should say yes, *please*.' Marianne widened her eyes at Prue.

Prue nodded. 'I agree. Thank you very much indeed. We're delighted to accept.'

Lady Campbell-Gryce beamed. 'If you tell me where you'd like me to put the fabric, then I'll bring in the rest of it.'

'I'll help,' Hettie said.

'We all can,' Prue said.

As she followed the others out of the hall, Hettie saw her Ladyship hadn't been exaggerating when she'd said she had a carload. The back seats were packed with many coloured fabrics right up to the roof, as was the front passenger seat. There was enough material to keep them making clothes for many months to come.

After their tea break, the women of The Mother's Day Club resumed their work. The village hall filled with the sound of sewing machines whirring and the hum of chatter from those who could talk while they worked. Only now they had an extra person helping.

Hettie paused the tacking she was doing for a moment and glanced over to where Marianne was patiently showing Lady Campbell-Gryce how to unpick a worn garment so it could be reused to make something new. Her brow furrowed in concentration, her Ladyship was absorbed in tackling the unpicking herself. It was a sight Hettie would never have dreamed of seeing but these days so many things were not as they used to be. Everybody was being stretched out of their comfortable ways, challenged to do more — even Lady Campbell-Gryce!

The morning flew by and when Prue called out that it was a quarter to twelve and time for them to pack away, a groan went up from the women.

'Can't we have another 'alf 'our?' Gloria responded. 'I'd 'ave got these trousers finished by then and they could 'ave gone straight into the clothing depot ready to be loaned out.' She held up the pair she'd been working on so diligently all morning.

'And me with this,' Edith called out, pointing to the blouse she was sewing.

'I'm sorry, I wish we could, but we only have the hall booked till quarter past twelve and we need to clear everything away, pack up the tables and chairs and make sure it's tidy,' Prue said. 'We can do more work on them again at our next meeting.'

'I wish we 'ad somewhere we could leave things out and work on them whenever we 'ad time,' Gloria said. 'Think of 'ow much more we'd get done then.'

'I know,' Prue said. 'But this is what we have, so come on, let's get packed up.'

Hettie had to agree with Gloria. It was a nuisance to have to set out and pack away at the start and end of each session but, with the village hall needed for so many other groups, what choice did they have?

CHAPTER 42

It was the smell that hit Prue first. A mixture of tobacco and the Brilliantine cream that Victor had used so liberally in his hair – the smell of her late husband. Prue halted in the doorway of his bedroom, with Gloria close behind her.

'Let's get the window open and let some fresh air in shall we? A room left shut up always needs a good blast through.' Gloria stepped past Prue, strode across the bedroom and heaved up the sash window, letting the gentle spring breeze into the room. 'There, that's better,' she said, turning with her hands on her hips and giving Prue an understanding look.

'Thank you, it was just I haven't been in here since he died and as soon as we opened the door, I could smell him.'

'Not him, ducks. Only the smell of the cigarettes he smoked and this.' Gloria picked up a tin of Brilliantine from the top of the chest of drawers. 'He himself ain't here to bother you anymore.'

Prue gasped, staring at her friend for a moment. Gloria had questioned in the past why Prue was married to such a man as Victor, thinking they didn't seem a likely couple. Did she know the whole story? 'I...' she began.

'I only know you weren't 'appy with him, Prue, I could see that. Now he's gone, you've got a chance to live your life your way and to be 'appy. Once we sort this lot out and send it off to new homes, it'll 'elp you move on.'

Prue nodded, her eyes filling with tears. 'I'm just going to check on Marie before we start.' Without waiting for a reply, Prue hurried along the landing, needing a moment to recover herself. Today would be difficult enough without digging deep into how unhappy her marriage had been.

Peeping in the door of what had been Edwin's room, and which was now shared by the two young sisters, Prue saw that Marie was still sleeping. It was the best thing for the little girl right now as she'd been up in the night again, crying with a stomach ache. Despite Nancy taking Marie to see the doctor yesterday, they were still no nearer to knowing what was the matter with her. He hadn't been able to find anything wrong and had prescribed rest and simple foods for the time being. Since Prue was going to be at home all afternoon, she'd volunteered to watch over Marie so Nancy could go to work for a few hours, trying to make up for having so much time off from Rookery House last week.

Squaring her shoulders, Prue returned to Victor's room and was relieved when she went inside that the fresh air was already working wonders, the smell of Victor already fading.

'Is Marie all right?' Gloria asked, stepping back from where she'd opened wide the doors of the dark-walnut wardrobe.

'She's still sleeping, bless her.' Prue stepped in front of the wardrobe. 'Right, let's get started.' She indicated the shirts, trousers and jackets precisely lined up on the rail, all hung in groups of clothing type. It was so typical of Victor's orderly, organised ways.

'You sure you don't want to keep anything for our village clothing depot? It could be repurposed into clothes for children?' Gloria asked as she took out a shirt and folded it.

'No, I'd rather not. We've got the large donation of material from Lady Campbell-Gryce to use. I know that won't last for ever and it seems silly when we could make good use of this stuff but...' Prue crossed her arms over her body. 'It really is best going somewhere I won't see it again.'

'I understand.' Gloria put her hand on Prue's shoulder. 'You've got to do what you're comfortable with. The WVS depot will be pleased, I'm sure, and so will whoever finally gets to wear them.'

While Gloria took out shirts and folded them neatly into piles on the bed, Prue removed the jackets. She needed to check through the pockets in case Victor had left anything in them. Delving into the pocket of a Harris tweed jacket which had been a favourite of his, her fingers felt the small familiar shape of a train ticket. Prue pulled it out and saw that it was dated a few weeks ago, from Great Plumstead to Norwich. He must have bought it to go and see his mistress. An image of Miriam Roper lying in her hospital bed flashed into Prue's mind and a wave of pity filled her, thinking how the woman had been so badly deceived by Victor.

'What 'ave you found?' Gloria's voice broke into Prue's thoughts.

'Just an old train ticket.' Prue held it up for her friend to see. 'Nothing interesting.'

'No secret stash of money, then?' Gloria gave a throaty laugh.

'No, not yet.' Prue raised her eyebrows. 'Victor was rather too particular about his money. I doubt very much there's any left lying around. He preferred it safely in the bank.'

'I can imagine. Right, I've finished the shirts. Shall I start on the pullovers? Do you want to send them to Norwich or we could pull them out at The Mother's Day Club and use the wool to knit new garments?' Gloria suggested.

'No, I'd rather they go to the WVS depot in Norwich, along with everything else.' Prue folded up the jacket and reached into the wardrobe for Victor's best suit.

Gloria nodded. 'Fair enough.'

Half an hour later, the bed was covered with neat piles of clothing sorted into type, from shirts to trousers, belts, pullovers and socks. They'd tied string around the bundles of clothes and put pairs of shoes with laces knotted and the belts linked together into a cardboard box.

Prue checked the drawers and wardrobe for any stray items and, satisfied that they'd gathered and sorted everything of Victor's, she felt a sense of relief. 'That's it. Thank you for helping. Having you here made it so much easier.'

Gloria threw an arm around Prue's shoulders. 'I'm glad to 'elp. What are you going to do with this room now?'

'Give it a thorough spring clean, move the furniture and I was even wondering about giving it a fresh lick of paint if I can get hold of some. Brighten it up.' Prue looked around the dark room, which would benefit from lighter-coloured walls. 'There's no rush. I need to sort Victor's study out next.'

'If you want any 'elp with that, let me know,' Gloria offered.

'Thank you, I might just take you up on that. Now if we can carry this lot downstairs and load it into my car, ready to take into Norwich on WVS business, then how about we have a sandwich?' Prue picked up the box of shoes and belts.

'Sounds like a good idea.' Gloria tucked a pile of shirts and another of pullovers under her arms. 'Lead the way.'

. . .

'Can you go up and see if Marie's awake and find out what she'd like in her sandwich — fish paste or spam?' Prue asked Gloria after they'd loaded the last of Victor's things into the car. 'What would you like?'

'I'll have spam, please,' Gloria replied. 'I'm 'ungry after all that sorting out.'

'It will be ready for you by the time you come down.' While Gloria returned upstairs, Prue went into the kitchen, washed her hands, and was cutting slices off the loaf of National wholemeal bread from the local bakers when she heard Gloria calling Marie's name, followed by loud footsteps hurrying down the stairs.

'I can't find Marie!' Gloria said, bursting into the kitchen. 'She ain't in her bedroom or the bathroom.'

'Are you sure?' Prue dropped the knife onto the bread board, her heart picking up its pace. 'She could be hiding somewhere.'

'Let's have another look. Maybe she's feeling better and playing hide and seek,' Gloria said in a hopeful voice. 'Perhaps I just panicked when she wasn't in her bedroom.'

'You have a look downstairs, check behind the sofa, under tables, just in case she's hiding there. I'll look upstairs.' Prue patted Gloria's arm encouragingly as they headed out of the kitchen.

Leaving Gloria to check the sitting room, Prue went upstairs, hoping that the little girl couldn't have gone far and was just playing hide and seek like the boys and Alice used to do. But after a thorough search of all the upper rooms, checking in wardrobes, under beds and in cupboards while calling out Marie's name, there was still no sign of her. A heavy feeling was growing in Prue's stomach. Nancy had left her looking after Marie and now the little girl was missing.

Prue made her way downstairs to the hall where Gloria stood waiting. 'Any luck?'

'No sign of her. Is that hers?' Gloria pointed at the navy-blue child's coat hanging on the stand in the hall.

'Yes. And her shoes are still there.' She gestured at the pair of brown girl's lace-ups that stood neatly paired near the skirting board. 'We'd better try the garden next…' She paused, noticing that the door under the stairs was slightly ajar. 'Did you open that?'

'No, what's in there?' Gloria asked.

'The cellar. Do you think…?'

'There's only one way to find out,' Gloria said. 'If she ain't down there, then we'll search the garden.'

Prue switched on the light just inside the cellar door and led the way down the steep concrete steps into the dimly lit space beneath the house.

'Marie!' Prue called out as she reached the bottom of the steps. 'Are you here?'

She thought there was a soft whimper and turned to Gloria. 'Did you hear that?'

Gloria raised her voice. 'Marie! Are you there, ducks? Are you all right?'

This time a howl filled the cellar, followed by sobs. 'She's over there.' Prue led the way to the area where they sheltered during air raids and where some camp beds had been set up. Curled up on top of one of them was Marie. A wave of relief swept through Prue. The little girl was safe although clearly distressed.

'It's all right, everything's all right.' Prue crouched down beside the camp bed and put her hand gently on Marie's shoulder. 'We were worried when you weren't in your room. What are you doing down here?'

'I was dreaming... there was an air raid,' the little girl managed between sobs. 'Bombs might fall on us.'

'There ain't no air raid going on, ducks,' Gloria said gently. 'It was just a bad dream.'

'If a bomb falls on here, we'll get killed like Victor was,' Marie said, her sobs already subsiding to sniffles.

'But that was in Norwich in a big raid. We don't get them out here in the countryside.' Prue took hold of Marie's hand.

'A bomb fell at Rookery House where my mum works,' Marie said.

'Have you been worrying about that, ducks?' Gloria asked.

Marie nodded.

Prue glanced at Gloria, who raised her eyebrows, a knowing look on her face. 'Has it given you tummy aches, do you think?'

Marie nodded again. 'But Mum's gone there today and a bomb might fall again and she'll be killed.'

'Most bombs fall on cities and at night-time. It's very rare to have one fall in the countryside,' Prue reassured the little girl, 'and if there is a raid, then we get to the shelter. We come down here, don't we?'

'But the house could be bombed, like what happened to Victor. George and Betty go in their Anderson shelter. It's safer.' Tears welled up in Marie's eyes again and she wrapped her arms tightly around her middle. 'My tummy hurts.'

Prue's eyes met Gloria's.

'Let's get you out of here.' Gloria bent down and picked the little girl up and with Marie holding fast around her neck, she carried her up the steps and out of the cellar.

Walking behind them, Prue mulled over what Marie had said. Victor's death in the Norwich Blitz, followed by the falling of the bomb at Rookery House had badly affected

Marie. The little girl's worry about them being bombed while sheltering in the cellar was something that Prue had thought about herself. Though it was far less likely to happen here than in Norwich but if it did... then they'd be buried under the house. Victor had refused to pay for an Anderson shelter in the garden saying the cellar was perfectly adequate, but he wasn't here anymore. It was time to put things right for everyone's sake, especially Marie.

Following Gloria into the sitting room, where she'd laid the little girl on the sofa, Prue sat down on a nearby chair and took hold of Marie's hand.

'I've been thinking that we should have an Anderson shelter of our own out in the garden, just like they have at Rookery House. What do you think?'

The look of relief that washed over Marie's face answered Prue's question. 'Yes please,' Marie said. 'Thank you, Auntie Prue.'

'Now how's your tummy feeling?' Prue asked.

'Better, it's not hurting,' Marie said, rubbing her stomach.

'Good, could you manage a sandwich, do you think?'

'Yes please.'

'How about I read to you while we wait?' Gloria suggested, picking up a children's book from the table nearby.

Marie shuffled along the sofa making room for Gloria to sit down beside her.

Leaving Gloria reading to the little girl, Prue went into the kitchen to finish making the sandwiches, relieved that the brief emergency was over. On the plus side, she thought, at least they now knew what was causing Marie's unusual stomach aches and clinginess to Nancy over the past week or so. The little girl had bottled up what she'd seen and heard about and was understandably frightened. With some easy adjustments, like getting an Anderson, hopefully Marie would be reassured and things could return to normal. Prue would let Nancy know everything as soon as she returned from Rookery House that evening.

CHAPTER 43

'She's perfectly fine this morning, like the old Marie,' Nancy said, placing a bunch of radishes that she'd just pulled up in the basket.

'No more tummy aches?' Thea asked, brushing soil off the roots of the radishes she'd just harvested, ready to take to Barker's shop in the village. She had listened in amazement as Nancy had recounted what had happened at Prue's house yesterday while she'd been at work here.

'Marie's not complaining of anything at all! She's eating well and seems to be completely back to normal. It's like a weight's been lifted off her shoulders. And mine!' The relief on Nancy's face was plain to see. 'Marie's been as happy as can be since Prue told 'er that she's ordered an Anderson shelter and it will be put in on Saturday.'

'All that worry made her ill, poor little girl,' Thea said sympathetically. 'I'm glad you've finally found out what was wrong. It shows how much the children take in and then fret about. Prue never liked sheltering in the cellar either but Victor...' she frowned, 'he wouldn't spend his money on a shelter. I remember the day we had ours put in – it was the day war was declared. Prue's boys helped Reuben dig out the hole and put the shelter together. They wanted one at home too but knew they'd have to make do with the cellar because their father had said no.'

'Things are changing now Victor's not 'ere anymore. And for the better,' Nancy said, tugging up more radishes.

'They certainly are,' Thea agreed.

'With Marie settled again, it means I'm back at work, only...' Nancy hesitated, idly turning the radishes she was holding around in her hand. 'It's made me think about 'ow I let you down badly when she was unwell, so perhaps I ain't the right person for this job. I love it, but you need someone you can rely on all the time. Someone without other responsibilities who wouldn't let you down at the last minute.'

'Marie couldn't help being unwell and now we understand why and that's being fixed.'

'I know, but Marie or Joan could catch something and be poorly again. Mumps, measles, influenza...' Nancy shook her head. 'Children often get ill and it's my job to look after them when that 'appens. I can't be in two places at once and I 'ate letting you down.'

'I've no complaints about your work, Nancy. You're keen to learn, work hard and do well. I understand what you're saying though.' Thea paused for a moment. 'Is there a way around this?'

'Maybe if I worked part time,' Nancy suggested. 'But that would leave you short and you'd not be able to get everything done.'

'Or you could work full time when you can and then if the girls need you, then you can see to them. Perhaps I could find someone else to step in and help if needed.'

'Really?' Nancy's eyes widened. 'You'd put up with a sometimes unreliable worker?'

'I wouldn't put it like that because when you're here, you are an excellent worker. You just require a bit more flexibility. I don't want to lose you, Nancy.' Thea smiled at her friend.

'Thank you ever so much!' Nancy threw her arms around Thea and gave her a tight hug. 'You and your sister are the best of women.'

'Thank you,' Thea said, laughing as Nancy released her. 'We've never been called that before.'

'Well, it's true. You and Prue 'ave made an enormous difference to me and my girls. It was a lucky day for us when Prue gave us a 'ome when we arrived here from London.'

'You and all the other mothers and children from London have made a considerable difference to Great Plumstead too,' Thea said. 'The first group of expectant mothers raised a few eyebrows to start with, but now it feels like everyone's part of the village and has been here for ages.'

'It feels like an 'ome away from 'ome. If we can't be in London, then this is the best place to be. Now,' Nancy said, 'how many more radishes do we need, do you think?'

As they returned to harvesting vegetables for the delivery to Barker's, Thea thought about what they'd talked about. Having children to care for was part of who Nancy was and Thea had to accept that. There would be times when Nancy had to be with them at home, but she was a good worker while she was here. If Thea could find someone to fill the gap when necessary, then there was no reason Nancy shouldn't remain working at Rookery House.

CHAPTER 44

'It's too far for her to get home on such a wee length of leave,' Elspeth said. 'Forty-eight hours isn't enough when you've a long way to go to travel there and back again. I know I couldn't get back to Scotland and return to the aerodrome in time.'

'So what's your friend going to do next week?' Hettie asked the young Waaf who'd popped round to Rookery House on her afternoon off.

'She's not going anywhere for her leave. Helen says she'll stay at the aerodrome and relax. But that's not much of a break with the rest of us in our hut having to be up at the usual time.' Elspeth took a sip of her tea. 'But it is what it is, I suppose.'

'You know, if that happens to you, then you can always come here and stay in the dining room,' Hettie offered. 'At least you'd get away from the aerodrome for a while, have some home-cooked food and a change of scene.'

Elspeth gave her a look of amazement. 'Thank you, that's so kind and I appreciate the offer!'

227

'Same applies for Marge,' Hettie added. 'Although with her coming from Kenilworth, she's not got as far to travel as you. But tell her anyway.' She paused, considering for a moment. 'I'm wondering if there isn't something that can be done in the village to help other Waafs who can't get home and back in the short leave they're given. Let me think about it.'

Elspeth nodded. 'I will, and thank you, again. Now tell me about this UXB you had here.'

'How did you know about that?'

'Someone heard in the village shop and told someone else on the aerodrome. You know how word soon spreads!'

'Well, it was a shock when Thea came in and said the children had found a bomb in the hay meadow...' Hettie began to recount what had gone on at the weekend. She was just telling Elspeth about the arrival of the bomb squad when there was a tap on the back door.

Getting up from the table, Hettie opened the door and was surprised to see who was standing there, a bunch of orange marigolds mixed with sprigs of white lacy cow parsley in his hand.

'Ted!' Hettie gave him a welcoming smile. 'What brings you here?'

'I've come to bring you thanks on behalf of the Home Guard for feeding us so well while we were here guarding the UXB. I thought you might like these as a token of our appreciation.' He held out the flowers.

'How delightful! Thank you.' Hettie took the flowers, admiring them. 'They're beautiful and go together so well.'

'Cow parsley's such a lovely delicate flower and it fits nicely with the marigolds.'

'Do you have time for a cup of tea?' Hettie asked.

'That would be nice, thank you.'

'Come on in.' Hettie stepped to the side and ushered him to

the kitchen table. 'I've got Elspeth here. She's one of the Waafs who stayed with us for a few weeks while the women's accommodation was being finished on the aerodrome.'

After Hettie had put the flowers in a vase of water, introduced Ted to Elspeth and he was seated with a cup of tea in front of him and a slice of cake, the conversation turned once more to the UXB.

'Did you see the bomb after it was taken out of the hole?' Elspeth asked Hettie.

'I did once it was safely on the back of the lorry, ready to be driven away. Great big thing it was.' Hettie held her arms out wide to demonstrate. 'It was a 250kg one, so they said, and it lay there wedged in place with sandbags like some metal beast.'

'It was a heavy job hauling it out of the ground, but the bomb squad knew what they were doing,' Ted said. 'They've had a lot of practice to get it right.'

'It's terrible to think of the damage a bomb can do if it explodes. We were lucky it didn't.' Hettie took a sip of her tea. 'Let's talk about something nicer than bombs. Tell me what brought you back to live in Great Plumstead after all this time, Ted?'

'My wife died a few years ago and then, after I retired, I felt like a change. I wanted to return to a familiar place and my sister had been widowed and asked me to live with her at Ivy Cottage,' Ted explained. 'It's good to be back in the village again after so many years. Things have changed what with the new aerodrome and a lot more people living here, but I like it. The Home Guard welcomed me in as I was in the platoon where I lived in Suffolk, so knew the drill.'

'Do you have any children?' Elspeth asked.

Ted shook his head. 'No, we were never blessed with them. Hilda's the only family I have left now.'

'I think you made the right decision to come back to live here in Great Plumstead,' Hettie said.

The conversation flowed between them on various topics for the next hour, with much laughter and good cheer. By the time the teapot was drunk dry it was half past three.

'I'd better get going.' Ted stood up. 'Thank you very much for an enjoyable time and the tea and cake, Hettie.' He gave her a wide smile, his eyes crinkling at the sides. 'It was good to meet you, Elspeth.'

'And you too,' Elspeth replied.

Hettie got up to see him out. 'Thank you for coming and for the flowers.'

Ted gave a small bow of his head. 'My pleasure. Goodbye then.'

After Hettie had closed the door behind him and returned to her seat at the table, she noticed Elspeth had a knowing look on her face.

'What's the matter?' Hettie asked. 'You look full of mischief.'

'If I'm not mistaken Hettie, I think you've got yourself an admirer there. And a very nice one too!'

'Don't be daft,' Hettie protested, batting her hand as if swatting away the idea.

'I'm not,' Elspeth said, her expression earnest. 'I think he likes you very much. He could hardly take his eyes off you.'

Hettie's cheeks grew warm, her gaze drifting to the vase of flowers that Ted had brought her which she'd stood in the middle of the table. 'I'm too old for that sort of thing.'

'No one's ever too old for love,' Elspeth said.

'I think you're getting ahead of yourself,' Hettie scolded. 'All Ted did was bring some flowers on behalf of the Home Guard as thanks for the food we provided.'

Elspeth let out a laugh. 'If you say so, but my instinct is that he rather likes you. Time will tell.'

Hettie rolled her eyes. 'You young women watch far too many films at the pictures which put romantic notions in your head.'

But what if Elspeth was right? a little voice whispered in Hettie's head. Ted was a lovely man, quiet, kind and gentle. How would she feel about it, if he *was* admiring of her? She couldn't give an answer because she didn't know and wasn't going to waste any more time pondering over it.

'Come on, Elspeth, you can put that energy of yours into helping me peel some potatoes rather than coming up with daft ideas.' Hettie stood up, grabbed her apron from its hook and handed another one to the young woman to put on over her uniform. 'I hope you'll stay for tea.'

'I'd like that very much, thank you,' Elspeth said, tying on her apron. 'And I'm sorry if I offended you.'

'You didn't.' Hettie's eyes met Elspeth's and she chucked. 'But I'm too old and have seen enough in life to jump to any far-fetched and silly notions.'

CHAPTER 45

Today felt like a day of changes, Prue thought, looking out through the kitchen window at the progress the men were making as they put up the new Anderson shelter in the back garden. Once it was built, it would be kitted out with bunk beds on either side to make it more comfortable for whenever they had to spend time in there. Importantly, having the shelter in place would reassure Marie.

Prue turned away from the window and steeled herself to face this morning's unpleasant task – the sorting through of Victor's study. She'd nipped in there earlier and opened the window, lifting and lowering the sashes as far as they would go to let fresh air inside the room.

Gloria was due to arrive to help in an hour's time, but Prue had planned to make a start on her own to go through the desk. She wasn't sure what she might find in there and so thought it best to tackle it while she was alone. There might be evidence of Miriam Roper somewhere and if there was, then it was better that Prue discover it — and keep it to herself.

Reluctant as she was, there was no point in putting it off any longer. Prue took a deep breath and headed through the hall into Victor's study. The fresh air blowing in had taken the edge off the stuffy smell of tobacco, but there was still an odour of cigarette smoke which no doubt had permeated the furniture, carpet, books and everything else. For now, Prue would have to put up with it, but once the room was sorted out and cleared, she'd make sure any lingering smell was banished, even if she had to scrub it out herself. She knew there was a lovely wooden parquet floor under the old carpet that would look lovely cleaned and freshly polished.

She sat down at the large desk, pulled out the top drawer and let out a laugh at the tidiness of it. Everything inside was neatly ordered in typical Victor style, the pens all lined up and not a stray paper clip in sight. At least it would make sorting it out easier, she thought. Prue got to work, going through the contents of the drawers and putting them into two boxes that she'd placed on top of the desk. One for items to keep which would be useful in the house, such as scissors, pens, pencils and other stationery; the other box for items that were linked to the business and which she'd take to the shop in Wykeham where they could go in the office. Things like ledgers which Victor had poured over so assiduously to make sure his pounds, shillings and pence all added up.

As she worked through the six desk drawers, Prue found nothing about Miriam Roper at all. Not a letter or a photograph of her. Nothing. It was as if she didn't exist. Considering this was a private room which Victor kept locked when he wasn't in here, it would have been the perfect place for him to have a photo of her tucked away, knowing it wouldn't be discovered. But there wasn't anything in here that wasn't connected to his business in some way.

Finishing the last drawer, Prue leaned back in the chair

and couldn't help feeling sorry for Miriam, because it seemed that Victor hadn't rated his relationship with his mistress as highly as she'd been led to believe. But that had been Victor all over, he had always put himself first.

Prue stood up. She wasn't going to dwell on Victor's deeds anymore, she had work to do. She turned her attention to the bookshelves and sorted through record books going back over many years. She gave each one a quick check through, flipping through the pages for anything hidden inside. She'd made good progress by the time Gloria arrived to help.

'It looks like you've done most of the sorting,' Gloria said, looking around the room. 'What do you want to do next?'

'I'd like to roll up this carpet and take down the curtains, then start with the cleaning, if you're still willing.'

'I certainly am!' Gloria agreed. 'I've come ready to work.' She put a hand on the hip of her flowery dungarees and patted her head, her platinum-blonde hair hidden under a scarf to protect it.

'We make a good pair,' Prue said, gesturing at her own dungarees, which were the ones Alice used to wear for work and that Prue now wore for doing jobs like this one or at the allotment.

They ferried the piles of ledgers and books out to Prue's car and then moved furniture around so they could roll up the large carpet which covered most of the floor.

'What are you going to do with this room?' Gloria asked as they stopped for a rest once the carpet was in a neat roll at one end.

'I've been thinking about it. First, it needs a good scrub and I prefer this parquet flooring.' Prue ran the toe of her shoe over the wooden floor. 'It's much more practical for what I've got planned in here.'

'And what's that?'

'Well, I wasn't sure at first, but now I've decided to use it for something quite special.'

'Go on, tell me,' Gloria urged her.

'It was you who gave me the idea.'

Gloria looked surprised. 'Me?'

'Do you remember what you said on Monday at The Mother's Day Club at the end of our clothes-making session? About how you wished we had somewhere where we could leave out our sewing and come back to work on it whenever we wanted?'

Gloria nodded. 'I do. It's frustrating 'aving to pack things away each session. Wastes so much time that we could be using to sew.'

'Exactly. So I thought, why don't we use this space?' Prue gestured with her arm. 'Turn it into a Mother's Day Club workroom. We can set up tables, have sewing machines ready to use and there's plenty of storage space for materials.'

Gloria's mouth fell open in surprise. 'The Mother's Day Club using Victor's old study!' She whooped, her eyes dancing with delight. 'It's a smashing idea. I love it!'

'I'm glad you think so. It's a perfect use of this room and filling it with women chatting and laughing while they work will be a welcome contrast to how it's been in here for so many years.'

'What would Victor say about it?'

'Oh, he'd disapprove, no doubt about it!' Prue laughed. 'But this is my house now and I want to share it with others. In fact, I've also decided to use his bedroom as a place where Waafs can come and stay for their leave, if it's too far for them to get home and back in the time they've been given. Hettie telephoned me last night to ask if there's anything I could do to help.'

'You're a very generous and kind person, Prue. You help so many people.'

'I'm only doing what I can, that's all. You do the same.' Prue said modestly. 'Will you help me take the curtains down now and we can hang them on the washing line and give them a good bashing to get any dust out before I wash them?'

'Let's do it,' Gloria said enthusiastically. 'I can't wait to have this as our Mother's Day Club workroom. What a difference it's going to make.'

'I hope so,' Prue agreed, thinking it would also make a tremendous transformation for her personally, helping to rid this room of the memory of Victor and the many unpleasant conversations she'd had in here with him over the years. 'It's a new start for this room and for me.'

Gloria clapped her hands. 'It's going to be wonderful in here. It really is!'

CHAPTER 46

It was the last Saturday in May and the day of the official opening of The Mother's Day Club workroom. Over the past week the room that had once been Victor's study had undergone a transformation.

After word had got out about the new workroom, offers to help get it ready had poured in. Members of The Mother's Day Club had volunteered to come and help, as well as Thea and even Lady Campbell-Gryce. The volunteers had worked hard helping to clean and move furniture, wash down walls and give the whole room a fresh coat of seashell-pink paint, which her Ladyship had donated, saying a spare unused tin had been found at the Hall and she wanted it put to good use.

Prue stood in the doorway, looking around the room, hardly able to believe the change. Gone was the sense of heavy foreboding she'd always felt every time she entered it to speak to Victor. No longer was it a place to be kept locked and only used by him.

Now it was bright and airy with the warm seashell-pink walls and it smelt of beeswax polish and lavender bags. New curtains with blue forget-me-not flowers on a rose-pink background stirred in the gentle breeze coming in the open window. Donated by Sylvia, Gloria's landlady, the pretty curtains were a welcome replacement for the dull green ones that used to hang there. Those were now washed and lay neatly folded on a shelf waiting to be reused and made into garments for the clothing depot.

Victor's old desk now stood against one wall with two sewing machines on top. Its drawers were provisioned with scissors, filled pin cushions, needle cases, spools of thread, tape measures, knitting needles and wooden mushrooms for darning. His old filing cabinet contained pattern pieces for making garments, instead of invoices and receipts.

One wall had shelves and cupboards for storing fabric and wool. Along the two other walls were long worktables, with another collapsed underneath which could be brought out and set up in the middle of the room when it was needed. Underfoot the wooden floor — after much scrubbing and polishing — now glowed a warm honey colour. It not only looked good but would be practical for sweeping up threads and snips of material.

'Are you ready? It's almost ten o'clock,' Nancy said, coming to stand beside Prue in the doorway.

Prue turned to her friend. 'Just taking a last look. Isn't it wonderful — and such a change for the better!'

'And it's going to be buzzing shortly. There are people out there keen to get started.' Nancy gestured towards the front door where they could see shadowy figures through the stained glass.

'Then we mustn't keep them waiting!' With a last glance at the wholly transformed workroom, Prue went to the door and, as she opened it, a loud cheer went up from the women who were eager to get started.

'Welcome everyone!' Prue was delighted to see so many familiar faces from The Mother's Day Club. 'Come on in and make yourselves at home.'

Gloria, who was first in line, called out. 'Let's get to work, ladies!'

Prue ushered the women inside, many of whom had been here earlier in the week helping to prepare the room. Each of them had invested time and effort into this new venture.

She was just about to close the door when a car drew up at the gate and Lady Campbell-Gryce stepped out.

'Good Morning, Prue,' she called. 'I've brought a little something for the new workroom.'

She opened the back door of her car and took out a tabletop wireless, the walnut wood casing shining in the sunshine.

Prue hurried over to help carry it in between them. 'This is very generous of you, thank you.'

'I thought it would be lovely to have some music or other programmes to entertain us while we work. I hear workers in factories enjoy listening to the Home Service while they make parts for engines or whatever. We can do the same as we sew!'

By the time *Music While you Work* started on the newly set up wireless at half past ten, the workroom was a hive of activity. Gloria was seated at the desk in Victor's old chair, stitching a little dress together on a sewing machine, while Edith worked at the other machine beside her. Nancy and Hettie were seated on chairs brought in from the kitchen, darning some of the latest batch of socks from the aerodrome and Lady Campbell-Gryce was learning how to cut out patterns with Marianne. The other women were gathered around the tables busy unpicking used garments and sewing on buttons.

Prue hummed along to the music as she sewed a hem on a skirt. A feeling of warmth and happiness filled her as she worked alongside her friends. This room was here for any of them to use whenever they had time. It was going to make an enormous difference to how much they could make, do and mend for the clothing depot.

Just then, *You Are My Sunshine* came onto the wireless and Gloria burst into song to accompany it. Prue and the other women quickly joined in, their combined voices filling the room with the joyful tune. It made Prue's heart soar to sing along to this happy song with her friends around her. Just a couple of months ago she would never have imagined something like this could ever happen in this room. It would have seemed an impossibility.

So much had changed in the past few weeks. Her life had altered in a dramatic and unexpected way but it had turned out mostly for the good. She was forging ahead with a new future and she wasn't alone, with wonderful women like these beside her and supporting her. Today was just the start of the new life that lay waiting for her.

Dear Reader,

I hope you enjoyed reading *Home Comforts at Rookery House* and seeing Prue's life change dramatically for the better. I had this in mind for Prue since the start of the series, and still have more plans for her yet!

Prue, Thea and Hettie and the other residents of Great Plumstead will return next in a festive novella - *Christmas Carols at Rookery House.*

I love hearing from readers – so please do get in touch via:

Facebook: Be friends on **Rosie Hendry Books,** or join my private readers group - **Rosie Hendry's Reader Group**
X (Twitter): @hendry_rosie
Instagram: rosiehendryauthor
Website: **www.rosiehendry.com**

You can sign up to get my monthly newsletter delivered straight to your inbox, with all the latest on my writing life, exclusive looks behind the scenes of my work, and reader competitions.

If you have the time and would like to share your thoughts about this book, do please leave a review. I read and appreciate each one as it's wonderful to hear what you think. Reviews also encourage other readers to try my books.

With warmest wishes,

Rosie

IF YOU ENJOYED HOME COMFORTS AT ROOKERY HOUSE...

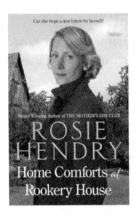

It would be wonderful if you could spare a few minutes to leave a star rating, or write a review, at the retailer where you bought this book.

Reviews don't need to be long – a sentence or two is absolutely fine. They make a huge difference to authors, helping us know what readers think of our books and what they particularly enjoy. Reviews also help other readers discover new books to try for themselves.

You might also tell family and friends you think would enjoy this book.

Thank you!

HEAR MORE FROM ROSIE

Want to keep up to date with Rosie's latest releases?

Subscribe to her monthly newsletter on her website.
www.rosiehendry.com

Subscribers get Rosie's newsletter delivered to their inbox and are always the first to know about the latest books, as well as getting exclusive behind the scenes news, plus reader competitions.

You can unsubscribe at any time and your email will never be shared with anyone else.

ACKNOWLEDGMENTS

A huge thank you to all my readers who have taken the Rookery House books and characters to their hearts.

Thanks to the fantastic team who help me create the books — editor, Catriona Robb and cover designer, Andrew Brown. Also to my author friends and especially those of the Famous Five whose friendship, chats and laughs together are such a joy.

Finally, thank you to David, who supports me in all I do.

Have you met the East End Angels?

Winnie, Frankie and Bella are brave ambulance crew who rescue casualties of the London Blitz.

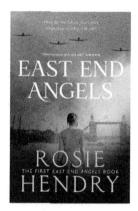

BOOK 1 - USA and Canada edition

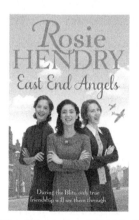

BOOK 1 - UK and rest world English edition

Available in ebook, paperback and audiobook.

BOOKS BY ROSIE HENDRY

East End Angels series

East End Angels

Secrets of the East End Angels

Christmas with the East End Angels

Victory for the East End Angels

East End Angels Together Again

Rookery House series

The Mother's Day Club

The Mother's Day Victory

A Wartime Welcome at Rookery House

A Wartime Christmas at Rookery House

Digging for Victory at Rookery House

A Christmas Baby at Rookery House

Home Comforts at Rookery House

Christmas Carols at Rookery House

Standalone

Secrets and Promises

A Home from Home

Love on a Scottish Island

A Pocketful of Stories

Rosie Hendry lived and worked in the USA before settling back in her home county of Norfolk, England, where she lives in a village by the sea with her family. She likes walking in nature, reading and growing all sorts of produce and flowers in her garden — especially roses.

Rosie writes stories from the heart that are inspired by historical records, where gems of social history are often to be found. Her interest in the WWII era was sparked by her father's many tales of growing up at that time.

Rosie is the winner of the 2022 Romantic Novelists' Association (RNA) award for historical romantic sagas, with *The Mother's Day Club,* the first of her series set during wartime at Rookery House. Her novels set in the London Blitz, the *East End Angels* series, have been described as 'Historical fiction at its very best!'.

To find out more visit **www.rosiehendry.com**

Printed in Great Britain
by Amazon

47472745R00148